IT WAS LIKE THUNDER ROLLING ACROSS THE SKY . . .

He heard it, faint at first but then louder and louder in only seconds, like History and Fate and other dark inhuman things coming after a man: a roaring crescendo of *Chimes*. First a few bells far away and then hundreds and more hundreds, all over Philadelphia—a pandemonium to knock you off your chair. And then the howling way up high in the wolf level, hundreds of agonizing dogs all complaining about what the chimes were doing to their sensitive canine ears—and still the chimes were louder than the dogs.

"You see?" Sigismundo said. "History is coming to get us. Will you kindly tell them the Italian gentleman prefers to play the piano in a brothel? *God save us all from history,"* he suddenly growled, and then he arose and tipped his cap and walked out.

I've met my share of strange birds, James Moon told himself, but this was the strangest yet. **The man regards history as his mortal enemy.**

NATURE'S GOD

Nature's God

Historical Illuminatus Chronicles

VOLUME 3

ROBERT ANTON WILSON

A ROC BOOK

ROC
Published by the Penguin Group
Penguin Books USA Inc., 375 Hudson Street, New York, New York
10014, U.S.A.
Penguin Books Ltd, 27 Wrights Lane, London W8 5TZ, England
Penguin Books Australia Ltd, Ringwood, Victoria, Australia
Penguin Books Canada Ltd, 2801 John Street, Markham,
Ontario, Canada L3R 1B4
Penguin Books (N.Z.) Ltd, 182-190 Wairau Road,
Auckland 10, New Zealand

Penguin Books Ltd, Registered Offices:
Harmondsworth, Middlesex, England

First published by Roc, an imprint of New American Library,
a division of Penguin Books USA Inc.

First Printing, June, 1991
10 9 8 7 6 5 4 3 2 1

 Roc is a trademark of New American Library, a division of

Penguin Books USA Inc.

Printed in the United States of America

△

When in the Course of human Events it becomes necessary for one People to dissolve the Political Bands
which have connected them with another, and to assume among the Powers of the Earth, the separate and
equal Station to which the Laws of Nature and Nature's God entitle them . . .

> —Thomas Jefferson
> Declaration of Independence
> of the United States

The question before the human race is, whether the
God of Nature shall govern the world by his own laws,
or whether priests and kings shall rule it by fictitious
miracles?

> —John Adams
> Letter to Jefferson, 20 June 1815

I only bow to Nature's God.

> —Philip Freneau, called the Poet
> of the American Revolution

△

CONTENTS

BOOK ONE

BOOK TWO

Book One

△

The world itself is the will to power—and nothing else! And you yourself are the will to power—and nothing else!

—Nietzsche
The Will to Power

△

1. Murder at Twilight

Clontarf 1014

Brian marched around Ireland constructing
simulated lunar craters

A Danish Norseman or Norwegian Dane named
Brodar, who wasn't particularly brilliant or scintillating and never did anything else that got into the history books, killed an old man around the hour of sunset
on April 23, 1014 in a bull-grazing field called Clontarf, on the north coast of Dublin Bay. Brodar, whatever elements of Danish and Norse were mixed in him,
was a Viking and he killed the old man with an axe
through the head. Vikings seem to have liked to kill
people with axes. Historians agree that, when not
combing the lice out of his beard or getting drunk,
your average Viking preferred to spend his time crack-
ing skulls with axes.

Incidentally, we know the Vikings spent a lot of time
combing lice out of their beards because archaeolo-
gists have made careful scientific catalogs of the Danish and Norse artifacts found around Dublin Bay, and
lice combs outnumber swords and all other imple-
ments of war about a hundred to one. As Sherlock
Holmes would tell you, "Observing thousands of lice
combs, one deduces the existence of many, many

lice." When the Irish said, "Here come those lousy
Vikings again," they were probably being literal.

I know the movie people left the lice out of that epic
adventure, *The Vikings*, starring Kirk Douglas and
Tony Curtis, but Hollywood has a tendency to glam-
orize things.

Although the historian Snorri Sturlusen has the kind
of name you would expect to belong to a troll in a
Norse myth, he appears to have been a real person,
and he left us our best records of the Viking invasions
or incursions in Ireland. All that the euphoniously titled Snorri chronicled about Brodar, besides his deed
of valor in the Clontarf field that memorable April day
in 1014—it was Good Friday, curiously—is that Brodar
was dark haired. The Irish tradition agrees, and calls
Brodar a *dhuv-gall,* which in Irish means "dark
stranger." The Irish never knew whether the invaders
were Norse or Danes, they just called them *dhuv-galls*
or *finn-galls* (dark strangers or blonde strangers) and
generally ran like hell when they saw them coming.

The old man who got Brodar's battle-axe through his
brain—he was sixty-four actually, but still blonde and
bursting with vinegar and venom, due to unusual
genes—was named Brian Caeneddi of Borumu, but is
usually remembered under the English version of his
name, which is Brian Boru. He was not the sort who
ran like hell when he saw the Vikings coming. In fact,
Brodar killed him in revenge, because Brian (Caeneddi) Boru had just defeated the Vikings again, which
was a nasty habit he had developed over the decades.
Brian Caeneddi (Boru), in fact, had been killing and
vanquishing Danes and Norsemen, all over Ireland,
for forty-six years, starting in 968 when, at the pre-
cocious age of eighteen, he had led a small band of
guerrillas to the Viking stronghold at Limerick, killed

every Dane and Norwegian in sight, and then burned the whole town down afterwards, leaving nothing behind but cinders.

That was just for starters.

During the next forty-six years, Brian marched around Ireland constructing simulated lunar craters— large smoking holes in the earth, full of charred bones and ashes—wherever the Vikings had previously had towns and strongholds. If Brodar hadn't axed him at sixty-four, Brian (Boru) Caeneddi might have gone on killing Danes and Norsemen for another ten or twenty years probably. Although much about that period of Irish history is clouded with legend and mystery, it is quite clear that Brian Boru had a distinct ethnic prejudice against Danes and Norsemen, or anybody with a Viking helmet on his head.

Some say one of these Scandinavian invaders had raped Brian's mother, others, that he was simply an early Sinn Feiner and believed in Ireland for the Irish.

Brian of Borumu was also politically ambitious, and, starting out as a local "king" or chieftain in the Shannon River valley, had made himself High King of Ireland by bribing all the other local "kings" who could be bribed (of which Ireland had God's plenty) and burying the ones who could not be bribed, and then persuading the previous High King, Malachi Ui Naill or O'Neill, to abdicate.

There are many different stories about how Brian Caeneddi persuaded Malachi O'Neill to give up the throne, and they are all incredible. The safest verdict is that Brian was a very persuasive talker, who could put even a radical idea like abdication across with enough unction and lubricating oil to make it go down smoothly, and besides, after Limerick, he never went anywhere without an army of about 500,000 loyal supporters.

After becoming High King, Brian Caeneddi of Borumu consolidated his genetic potential by marrying his sons and daughters into royal or noble families all over the British Isles and even in France. You've encountered his granddaughter in English Lit class; she was Lady Macbeth. The Caeneddi genes were actually carried by the later O'Neill kings, the royal Stuarts of Scotland and England, the Hapsburgs, the Lorraines, and, eventually, by the Hanovers, the Mountbattens and the Minority Whip of the U.S. House of Representatives, Tip O'Neill.

The name Caeneddi was by then spelled, English-fashion, Kennedy, and Brian Boru's pugnacious and charismatic seed had found its way to the presidency of the United States.

An axe in the skull can stop even a man like Brian Boru, but it does not stop the genetic vector in time of which he is an expression.

2. Rape Before Lunch

Lousewartshire 1776

The Union Jack hung proudly above the contest
of constitutional law and pure reason

The Italian Englishwoman or English *Italiana* who
was to overthrow the British Empire by 1950 did not
have any of Brian Boru's pugnacious genes, but she
was unknowingly carrying some of Brodar's, because
Brodar's clan had been among the Normans (Norse-
French) who overran Sicily in the eleventh century and
held parts of southern Italy, up to Napoli, off and on
for a few hundred years. This lady became a revolutionary on July 4, 1776, but that marvelous dating did
not surprise her when she noticed it later because she
lived always in a web of synchronicity.

Of course, back in 1776, Lady Maria Babcock had
no realization that she was becoming a revolutionary.
The very word, *revolutionary,* hardly existed in her
vocabulary, or anybody's. The strongest word of that
sort she knew was *rebel*, which was about one step up
from the Norway rat, and rebels did not make revo-
lutions, which signify basic change, but only insurrections, which signify a bloody but temporary nuisance.
Rebels, everybody knew, were all mad and were
quickly and efficiently apprehended and hanged
throughout the Empire On Which The Sun Never Sets,

and that was the normal end of their bothersome insurrections.

So Maria was not aware she was becoming a revolutionary, and certainly nothing in her twenty-six years had prepared her for such a role. She was, after all, Contessa Maldonado back in Napoli and a Lady of the Realm here in England. Her father, old Count Maldonado, was as liberal as was safe in Napoli, where the Holy Office of the Inquisition still had two spies in every household and one lounging by the lamppost on the corner; her husband. Sir John Babcock, was a Whig and therefore a bit of a philosophical radical—he thought Nature's God was Newton's ingenious clockmaker rather than the Bible's Hanging Judge.

But both men were within the norm for their time and their society. Maria thought she was within the norm, too, and had no idea that she was about to launch herself on a career that would destroy both the morals and the morale of the Christian world, undermine the backbone of an Empire, and reverse the trajectory of two thousand years of history. It wouldn't have stopped her if she had known. Maria Babcock was a feisty woman.

Maria's revolution began, like most of the popular novels of the time, with a dark, handsome, but enigmatic nobleman; a pious, dull, and frightened snip of a servant girl; and—naturally—a little casual rape before lunch. If Richardson had been a little more honest and less sentimental, the incident might have been the climax of *Pamela*.

The dark, saturnine, and (in this case) alcoholic nobleman was Sir Vaseline Foppe-Wellington; the sweet and pious victim was a housemaid named Justine Case. The trial occurred at the courthouse in Lousewartshire and Maria, Lady Babcock, was there by accident. She had been in London that morning to buy a present for her daughter, five-year-old Ursula, and had stopped in the town to get out of her carriage for a few moments—the hot July sun had turned the carriage into a plausible imitation of an ironmonger's oven, and Lousewartshire was a good place to rest and recuperate before the last twenty miles to Babcock Manor.

Maria had been reading a chryselephantinely overwritten book called *Moll Flanders* in the coach, and very definitely she thought the somber, passionate, tragicomic, and picaresque story was most absorbing, and certainly presented the dark, sinister, underground side of English life in a vivacious and veridical manner that carried conviction, but she wished Mr. Defoe were not so in love with ornamentally excessive adjectives and long, stentorian, and somewhat inchoate sentences that, even by the standards of the time, seemed to twist and turn through curlicues and arabesques and wind on and on through ever-increasing clauses and sub-clauses, including abrupt changes of subject and total *non sequiturs*, even if he did seem to be making a unique effort to understand a woman's perspective on the world, which was all to the good, of course, and it was less monochromatically monotonous (she had to admit) than the other one he wrote with virtually nobody in it but that one ingenious mechanic on the island, living in total isolation until he found that mute but ineluctable footprint; and yet it could all be told as well and be more pleasant to read if those sentences did not get so totally out of control and sprawl all over the page so often in positive apotheosis of the lugubrious style, and then she wondered if reading so much of such labyrinthine and arabesque prose for so long in the hot carriage had affected her own mind and she were starting to think like that herself, instead of just enjoying the shade of the oak trees and resting from thought in the dense cool quiet of the mid-afternoon English summer.

Unfortunately, there wasn't much to do in Lousewartshire. It was not only shady and silent and comparatively cool but also not much livelier than the specimens preserved in alcohol bottles at Oxford.

Maria wandered into the courthouse, as she had on a few other occasions, because the dramas played there were often as melodramatic and frequently as incredible as any Elizabethan or even Jacobean revenge tragedy on stage in London. Her husband, Sir John, himself often said that he had learned more of human nature and human psychology in small-town courthouses than in the Classics. Sir John liked to talk; that was why he was in Parliament.

"The Classics," John said, "are splendid and grandiose. Of course, of course. Um. But because they are sublime, they are therefore larger than life and more majestic. People in the Classics only commit murder for reasons that make sense. You have to go to a town courthouse to find out that most murders are committed because of a silly quarrel about somebody's dog barking at night or the theft of a small piece of goat cheese."

So Maria wandered into the courthouse, and tried not to respond visibly to the *ohs* and *ahs* when people noticed that the Lady of Babcock Manor, a relative of the mighty Greystokes, was present. She took off her fashionable blue bonnet—her long midnight-black Neapolitan hair, so Mediterranean and un-English, set off more murmers and mutters of awe—and attended to the drama on the stage.

The Divine Playwright that day provided Maria with a scene—the courtroom—that looked as if it might once have been new and maybe almost clean when Bonnie Prince Charlie had his first sip of Drambuie and hoisted his Royal Stuart tartan kilt for the first highland lass of his life.

Resplendent in red for courage, white for purity, and blue for honor, the Union Jack hung proudly above the contest of constitutional law and pure reason to be staged that day. Behind the bench was a blotchy, shadowy, imitation-Rembrandt portrait of George III that looked as if the artist had astigmatism. The cast on stage included a judge who looked so grossly obese, lard-headed, and brutal that he might have come straight to court from posing for a Hogarth etching; two barristers who were obviously altogether too clever by far; a Plantiff who was so tiny and timid and yet so pretty in a wan and undernourished way that she looked vaguely like every dull-normal servant girl who had ever been raped in English history; and Sir Vaseline Foppe-Wellington, the Accused, who was drunk as usual and totally unconcerned with the drama he had been compelled to attend, since he knew the ending in advance. He was dressed in the green silk then fashionable, with Italian (but not very clean) lace showing at the sleeves, and was sniffing some snuff, languidly, as if even that were a great effort and he would rather be home in bed.

The Plaintiff was giving evidence as Maria seated herself toward the back of the courtroom. Little skinny Justine was nervous as a presbyopic turkey in a dog kennel, but there were lines of anger and determination around her weak, pale lips. Her dress was scrubbed scrupulously clean but was so faded that Maria wondered what on earth her other dresses must look like, the ones she had rejected for that day.

The barrister questioning her—a youngish man for

that profession, but professionally and plausibly sincere as a card sharp—spoke sympathetically and gave her ample time to gather her wits between questions. Obviously, he had been appointed to act for the Crown.

"He put his hand all the way up, between your legs?" the barrister said, repeating the girl's last statement for emphasis. He sounded genuinely shocked, as if he hadn't read all the evidence in preparing for court.

"Yes, my lord." Justine was embarassed and flushed but still unintimidated.

"He touched your, um, private parts?"

"Yes, my lord. He tried to push his finger up into me. It hurt awful, the way he rammed that finger in me."

The barrister looked down at the floor, as if controlling terrible outrage, like a politician announcing proven felonies by the opposition party. "And this was only your second week in employment there?"

"Yes, my lord."

"You told the Court that you resisted. Specifically, how did you resist this brutal assault?"

"I struggled to get loose. I told him I would scream and his wife would hear. I scratched him. I scratched his face with my nails. Finally," Justine said with girlish simplicity, "I put my knee in his family jewels."

"And what did he do?"

"He gave me a sort of blow in the chest. He called me a stupid cow and went out of the room, all red in the face and holding his crotch and trembling. I was sure I would be sacked and my ma would be sore angry at me."

"Were you discharged, child?"

"Why, no, my lord. He pretended nothing had happened and left me alone after that, until—"

"Yes. Until the day of 16 June this year, was it?"

"Yes, my lord."

"Tell the court what happened on that day."

"He was more drunk nor usual."

The other barrister rose dramatically, like a blue whale surfacing suddenly. He was older, stouter, and had the ruddy complexion of a man who either enjoyed outdoor life on his farm or drank a bottle of brandy a day. "Objection, your lordship."

"Sustained," the judge said. "A servant cannot be considered a medical expert on degrees of intoxication."

The barrister for the crown made a gesture of despair, then sighed with resignation. Maria admired his talent. He understood this point of law as well as his colleagues, but he expressed—without words—the baffled impatience the jury must be feeling at what would seem pointless hairsplitting to them. In their nonlegal minds, plain honest merchants (or plain dishonest merchants) that they were, it required no expertise to say if a man was more drunk than usual. "Your master," the barrister for the Crown said carefully, "appeared intoxicated to you. Is that what you mean?"

"Yes, my lord. Even worse nor most days."

"Objection!"

"The witness will not offer opinions," the judge said testily. Maria suddenly thought he was exactly the physical type Shakespeare had in mind when creating Sir Toby Belch. Give him another five years of prime mutton and beer and he might even qualify to play Falstaff, if he learned how to smile without leering at the same time.

"Your master had taken drink," the crown barrister said quickly. "Did he attempt to fondle you again?"

"No, sir. I mean—"

"I understand. You mean that he simply seized you, is that it?"

"Objection. Leading the witness."

"Sustained. You know better than that, Mr. Drake."

"I apologize, your lordship. The sheer horror of this disgusting tale has distracted my reason."

"Objection! Now that is clearly prejudicial."

"An atrocity has been perpetrated and my learned colleague, with no more human compunction than a scorpion, insists on belaboring minute desiderata and total irrelevancies as if we were enquiring into the land title of a privy—"

"Objection! Mr. Drake is making speeches and enflaming the jury, since he knows Plaintiff has no case at all!"

"You will both stop this at once," the judge said sternly. "Those tricks may pass in some courts, but I will not tolerate them here. Proceed, pray God, in a more orderly manner, or you will both have cause to pray God most earnestly that contempt citations are not forthcoming." He seemed as righteously indignant as a preacher examining a disappointing collection plate.

Maria glanced at the jury. They were trying to look as expressionless as twelve eggs in a box, but she noticed that they were enjoying this ritualized cockfight even if they did not understand it.

But Maria also noticed—really noticed, for the first time in her life—that the jurors were all male.

Well, of course, English juries were all male, as all juries always were and as Parliaments was, and banking officers, and the reverend clergy. Maria had never speculated about that before. She reflected a great deal about God (who, in her opinion, was neither Sir John's Newtonian clockmaker nor the clergy's Hanging Judge but a passionate pilgrim) and she wondered endlessly about her own strange healing powers and she thought every day about the welfare of her children and the music of Mozart and Vivaldi, but she had never philosophized about the structure of the society in which she lived any more than she wondered about why mice were not as big as mules.

Now she also observed that some of the twelve eggs in the box were not totally expressionless. A few had mildly lascivious flickers in their eyes when they glanced at the Plaintiff.

But Drake, the crown barrister, was pushing on through the legal technicalities like a determined explorer cutting his way through dense and rubbery underbrush. "Tell us in your own words what happened that day," he said quietly.

"I was making up the beds, my lord. In the master bedroom, it was. He came up behind me and—"

"Clearly, now, by 'he' you mean the defendant, your employer, Sir Vaseline Foppe-Wellington."

"Yes, my lord. Himself."

"He came up behind you, and—?"

"He grabbed me from behind."

"Where did he place his hands upon your body?"

"On my breasts."

"On your *breasts*. Yes. You then did what?"

"I struggled and said I would scratch him again and tell his wife this time. My lord."

"And his response?" Drake asked quietly.

"He pushed me violently forward upon the bed and, and, *and* raised my skirts behind. My lord."

"Behind . . . You were prone then, rather than supine?"

"I beg your pardon, my lord?" Justine was unnerved by unfamiliar words.

"He pushed you forward from behind, you testified. You must have landed face down on the bed, I take it?"

"Yes, my lord." The girl was beginning to look more frightened, less determinded. Maria knew at once that the simple young thing—hardly more than a child—had never fully understood, emotionally, that she would have to tell *all* the details to an open court.

"You were prone and he raised your skirts behind, you told us. What happened then?"

"He pulled down my pantaloons and he, he, *he* put his thing into me."

Drake lowered his voice still further, like a whoremonger at a baptism. "Where did he, ah, put his male organ into your person?"

"In the bad place. Behind. The worst sin of all, my ma always told me."

A juror sneezed, explosively. It was almost a nervous reaction, and Maria realized how silent the room had become in the last few minutes.

Maria looked with curiosity at Sir Vaseline Foppe-Wellington, as one might look at something green and black with six legs found crawling behind the bathtub. He was engaged in pouring whiskey into his water glass, behind the table where the judge would not see. He appeared mildly bored, as if a persistent tradesman had presented a bill for the third time.

"He sodomized you," Drake said, putting pain in his voice. "Did he spend?"

"No, my lord. He couldn't. He was even more blind drunk nor usual, as I was trying to tell you before."

"He couldn't spend." Drake's voice was even softer. "He then gave up his abuse of you?"

"No, my lord. He said something like, 'Well, my

sweet, we will just have to try harder.' And he kept ramming his thing into me.''

"You were in great pain?"

"Not yet, my lord. His thing, he couldn't make it stay hard. He kept ramming me and saying 'now' and 'soon' but it never got hard really. It would start to get hard and then just flop around like a lawn hose.''

There was a muffled noise from the jury box. Somebody had almost laughed but succeeded in stifling it; the sound was like a swine gargling. The judge frowned, but said nothing.

"He kept 'ramming' you. For how long?"

"I don't know, my lord. It was a long time, I think."

"Did he succeed eventually in spending his seed? In this unnatural and libertine manner forbidden by Holy Writ?"

"He grew angry after a long time. He said, he said, he said, my lord,''—Justine almost wept then—''that I must turn over or he would strangle me.''

"Can you quote his exact words?"

"Objection," the defense barrister said. "Assuming this story is not a mere fabrication, as we suspect it is, the young lady would not be able to quote *exact* words. Her mind would be too shocked to recall specific words with accuracy.''

"Sustained," the judge said, after thinking about that for a moment. He looked as if he had been asked to explain the square root of minus one, Maria thought.

"In general," Drake said, "what was the content of defendant's threat to you?"

"He said I was a stupid bitch and he would wring my neck if I did not turn over and do what he told me.''

"You turned over?"

"He was very drunk and bloody angry. I was frightened out of my wits, my lord. I turned over."

"And then what did he do to you, child?"

"He he *he* ah *ah.*" The girl visibly trembled. "He didn't do what I expected. He made me take it in in in, he made me take it in in in my mouth."

"Was the brute able to spend then?"

"Objection. He knows better than that, your lordship." Defense council hardly raised his voice this time.

"Mr. Drake," the judge began. "Did they not teach you the rules of direct examination at Cambridge?"

"I apologize, your lordship." Drake turned back to Justine, as if with infinite patience." Was the *defendant* able to spend then?"

"He was not, my lord."

"How long did this second violation continue? Approximately?"

"Very long. Longer than when he was at my, my bottom. Your honor."

"I am not your honor," Drake said quickly. "Only the judge is to be so addressed. You are very upset, understandably, and this is a horrid tale. Are you able to continue?"

"Yes, sir. My lord."

"He attempted two abominable and unnatural acts upon you and did not succeed in spending. Do you think an hour had passed by then?"

"I believe so. It seemed an eternity."

"What did he attempt next?"

"He entered my cooney." The girl was now too dazed by the memories to be embarassed any longer. "That hurt worst of all. The membrane broke and I screamed. That's when he did strangle me."

"He choked you, violently. Did you stop screaming?"

"I think I fainted finally."

Somebody moved and a chair creaked. The sound
seemed as loud as a charge of Scotch horse soldiers
with bagpipes keening.

"When you awoke, what was transpiring?"

"He had turned me over once more and was at my
bottom again."

"Did he speak to you at this time?"

"He said it was my fault that he couldn't spend. He
said I was cold in the blood and inhuman. Then he
got his riding whip."

"He whipped you? Where?"

"On my bottom."

"Did he speak during this assault?"

"He said he would warm my blood and he started
praying to Jesus to make me a real woman, is what he
said. He kept saying Our Lord's name over and over."

"He kept saying Our Lord's name. The name Jesus,
you mean. This was while he was whipping you on the
buttocks?"

"Yes, my lord."

"He was whipping your buttocks and saying, *'Jesus, Jesus, Jesus'* over and over like that? *Jesus Jesus
Jesus Jesus Jesus* and whipping you?"

Sir Vaseline Foppe-Wellington took a refined little
sip of his whiskey-spiked water and dabbed his mouth
delicately.

"Yes, my lord."

"And then what happened?"

"He finally threw the whip aside and climbed upon
my body again. He put his thing in my bottom one
more time and it was hard enough by then to hurt me

and he groaned and gasped and seemed to spend then. He was all over bloody and so was I.''

"Yes, I can see that would be the case. After the monster had devirginated you and whipped you viciously, there would be much blood on both of your bodies. Did he speak again?''

"Yes, my lord. He said something I couldn't understand. I still don't understand it. He said, 'Admit you liked it, you little whore.' I'd been crying and screaming and scared to death and he wanted me to say I *liked* it.''

"You were both 'all over bloody' and he wanted you to say you liked it.'' Drake turned and grimaced, as if in loathing. Perhaps he really did feel that (as Maria did) but he was *performing* all the time. "Was that the end of your ordeal?''

"It was the end of what he done to me. He went to sleep then, full of the booze and all worn out, and I got out of that room. I got out of the house. I was still scared awful. I couldn't talk to the other servants. I couldn't go home and talk to my ma. I just kept running until I came to the sheriff's house. His wife, she held me while I told what happened. That's when I really started to cry—really cry, like a bairn. Before that I was too scared even to cry normal-like. It was only in her arms I could cry.''

Maria heard a long *a-a-a-a-a-h* sound and realized that Sir Vaseline had just yawned. He sipped his whiskey-water again.

Drake announced that the direct examination was concluded.

Council for the defense arose. Older, burlier, he stood for a moment beside Drake, looking like a weathered old bear thoughtfully deciding the quickest way to devour an upitty fox who had been playing

tricks on him. Then Drake sat and the old bear went
to work on young Justine Case, a housemaid who had
never been in a law court before.

The next three quarters of an hour turned Maria
Babcock into a revolutionary, but she was never able
to remember in detail all that had transpired. Drake,
it seemed she recalled, was on his feet every two minutes, objecting and objecting and objecting again. The
judge, Maria thought in memory, probably upheld
many of these objections—perhaps most of them. It
did not matter—the questions that were ruled "out of
order" and therefore went unanswered left an impression anyway. The jury looked both uncomfortable and
furtively lewd: There were no more stifled laughs, but
an odor of sanctified prurience clung over them, as if
they were being allowed to watch through the peep-
hole in a brothel, in order to write a report on vice for
a church enquiry.

Justine was being raped again, this time psycholog-
ically.

Council for the defense—his name was Hartford
Coke Bacon; Maria never forgot that—wanted to enquire into the "moral character" of the Plaintiff, as
evidence of her reliability; the judge ruled this was
permissible. Justine was asked if she had never had
sex with a boy in her whole life. Her denials were
subject to rhetorical ridicule—a farm lass who claims
to have reached sixteen years and hasn't gone up in
the hayloft with a boy *even once?* Did she expect reasonable men of the world like the jurors to believe
that? Well, did she never *kiss* a boy? And did she let
him touch her? She was sure about that? The laws of
perjury were read by the bailiff, at council's request,
and over Drake's objections that Plaintiff was being
badgered. Well, so she did kiss a boy once—and did

she allow the boy to touch her? Where? For how long? Was he the only boy? Two then? Was she sure there weren't three? Four? More? They only kissed her and touched her? Did she want to hear the perjury law read again to refresh her memory?

It went on. Had Justine ever *spent* while the boys were touching her? Did she understand that a girl does not literally spend seed like a man? Well, did she feel a warm rush all through her? Was she out of breath? A warm rush and out of breath, too, eh? And she didn't know that was spending and her ma hadn't told her it was mortal sin? Did her ma tell her anything about sin at all? And was she sure there were only two boys who took such liberties, not three or four or more? The young virgin does not seem so innocent anymore—and if she did spend on occasion, was it only from *touching?* She had testified that her employer was not "hard" for a long time—when had she seen a penis that was "hard?" How did she know that one grows hard during intercourse if she had never had intercourse? What were her standards of comparison— how many really hard penises had she seen or touched? She didn't touch the boys while they were touching her and making her spend? She didn't let either boy put it against her leg while touching her? Just for a few moments? Not between her legs? Would she explain again how she knew so much about what is "really hard" and what is only relatively hard?

It went on, and on, and on. Over increasingly vehement objections, the questions became more rhetorical—"All's fair in love, war, and cross-examination," a barrister had once explained to Maria. Wasn't it true that Plaintiff invented this whole story? Was she not pregnant by a farm boy? Had she not gone to her employer, the generous and liberal Sir Vaseline, in a crude attempt to blackmail him for money so she could hire a midwife to do an abortion? When he refused to give money for such a heinous crime, had she not sworn to get revenge by filing false charges of rape against him? Did she not understand that he had taken the stand and testified about her blackmail attempt and the jury would have to decide which of them was a liar under oath? Did she want the perjury law read again? And back to the boys who touched her, now we want the full truth, under penalty of perjury, had not a single one of all those boys done more than just touching?

After forty minutes, while Justine was in hysterics, Mr. Bacon was shouting at her to tell the truth—could she even *remember* which of her dozens and dozens of boys had made her pregnant with the child she had killed? Did she not invent the story of rape and whipping to explain the blood of the abortion?

Drake summarized the case for the Plaintiff. What the sheriff had testified about Justine's terrible emotional and physical condition when she arrived at his house. The doctor's testimony supporting her story of whipping. The obvious honesty of this frightened child who had been abused so viciously by both the defendant and his heartless barrister.

Bacon summarized for the defense. Could any jury of sober men believe one of these farm wenches about anything they said? Were these country girls not all notorious liars and thieves? Was it thinkable that a Peer of the Realm would do such vile and monstrous deeds? Would law and order be safe, would monarchy be safe, would England itself be safe, if a man of property and noble name could be convicted on the perjured testimony of a promiscuous little farm slut who had rolled in the hay with half the boys in three counties?

The judge explained to the jury that they had to be sure beyond a reasonable doubt that defendant had committed the abominable and unspeakable acts alleged. He made it sound as if any doubt was legally reasonable and he indirectly but distinctly managed to support defense's contention that any sentimental notion that the plaintiff, a mere servant, might be more honest than her employer would indeed jeopardize the entire social order. He spoke at length of the grave and serious doubts about the plaintiff's chastity raised during cross-examination, but in fairness he did remind the jurors of the doctor's testimony about injuries, adding, however, that they had to be sure beyond a reasonable doubt that she didn't inflict them herself to support her monstrous story.

Maria was white faced and shaken. It was like opening the cellar door in her home and finding the entire cast of *Titus Andronicus* had moved in last night.

The jury deliberated for five minutes.

When they came back, they found Sir Vaseline Foppe-Wellington not guilty. He yawned and took some more snuff.

Maria thought, Well, one could expect men of *property* to stick together. But then she thought, And one might also expect *men* to stick together.

An old woman, distinctly shabby, shuffled to the front of the courtroom and glared at Justine, then slapped her hard on the face.

"See, you damnation fool!" the old woman cried. "Nobody never believes *us* against *Them*. Didn't I tell you what would happen? And didn't you think you knew better than your old ma who has lived twice as long as you? Now you went and lost a good kip for nothing, and you'll never get another to feed us."

Even then Maria Babcock did not know that she had

embarked upon the path of revolution in the last few minutes of the trial.

She thought she was just going to write a sensible, if forceful, letter to the London *Gazette*. She was not going to demand a reform and overhaul of the entire legal system. She merely wanted to ask some serious questions about all-male juries.

She had no idea what that letter would unleash upon her. She did not know she had embarked on a path that would lead to the ultimate question in Western theology—namely, whether God Himself had a Willy.

The judge, who owed his appointment to Foppe-Wellington's influence, later that day sentenced an unemployed laborer to hanging, for the crime of stealing one loaf of bread. There was no reasonable doubt in that case, since the thief admitted his crime and offered no legal excuse for his felony, merely saying that he had been starving.

Sir Vaseline Foppe-Wellington was acquitted of similar rape charges twice in the next ten years, but eventually acquired paresis and spent his last days convinced he was the late King James II and his house was infested with Orange agents in wooden shoes attempting to poison him.

Maria hired Justine Case as an extra housemaid for Babcock Manor.

Hartford Coke Bacon was descended from both Lord Coke and Sir Francis Bacon, and he never missed a chance to let everybody know it. His American great-grandniece, Delia Bacon, impressed Emerson with her wit and brilliance, but is best remembered as the inventor of the thesis that her ancestor, Sir Francis Bacon, had collaborated with Sir Walter Raleigh in composing the plays attributed to the upstart crow from Stratford.

Drake was *not* descended from Sir Francis Drake but he was a collateral ancestor of Robert Putney Drake, who two hundred years later would acquire some remarkable Atlantean statues from a descendent of the madcap musician, Sigismundo Celine, who had wounded Maria's brother in a duel in Napoli in 1770.

Maria Babcock was still a happily married woman in 1776 because the man who had come from Ireland to England in 1771 to murder her husband had changed his mind when a rock fell out of the sky. That man, almost a murderer except for a coincidental rock, carried some of the seed of Brian Boru, by way of the "Southern" O'Neills of Leinster. We are about to meet him, in Philadelphia, where he is about to encounter the more desperate character who once shot Maria's brother and who is currently being hunted by assassins hired by the French royal family. There are wheels within wheels.

3. Revolution and Witty Sayings

Philadelphia 1776–Chicago 1968

A child's grief remembered
with gentle irony

It was so hot in Philadelphia on July fourth that everybody was mildly dizzy. Seamus Muadhen often thought, later, that the dizziness explained the mad thing the Continental Congress did that day, even if the booze explained the even madder thing he himself did.

But in the morning, wandering in the moist, mucky, totally maddening heat like a man trying to swim in gelatine, Seamus had only the foggiest notion that some new contraption called the Continental Congress existed at all, at all. He had come across Delaware Bay on the ferry from Baltimore to find a better job than the fishing boats offered—Christ, man, he had had enough of the fishing back in Dun Laoghaire, Ireland—and his attention was on the houses that looked rich enough to afford servants. Seamus had been in service to the Babcocks in England and it was altogether less nasty and damp and miserable and generally desperate than going after the bloody damned fish in the boats at ungodly hours when a landsman can still lie in bed and snore.

Seamus knew, of course, that the Continental Congress was considering What To Do About England, a subject that had once agitated himself when he was younger. It no longer agitated him. What To Do About England in his opinion was a question equal in imbecility to What To Do About the Law of Gravity. You either survived it or it bloody killed you. You couldn't *do* anything about it. The trees all over Ireland were decorated and festooned with the black, tarry bodies—tarred to preserve them, as a warning to others—of brave young fools who had thought there was something you could *do* about bloody England.

Seamus had the brightest brick-red hair in Philadelphia that day—red hair was a common trait back in Leinster, where he was born, due to the indefatigible energy of the royal O'Neills of Tara in generously spreading their noble seed, including some especially choice dominance genes from Brian Boru. Seamus also had a right eye that had lost most of its sight, due to something a British soldier had done to him once, and a persistent bad conscience, due to something he had done later to the British nobleman named Babcock who had employed him. And by the holy Paul and Peter and Patrick, in this infernal climate he also had by noon of the clock a thirst like Moses and all the host of the Israelites after forty years tramping back and forth all over the bleeding desert looking for the Promised Land.

Nobody in the grand houses wanted more servants; many of them, unknown to Seamus, were already considering fleeing to Canada. The heat was more hellish every hour and Seamus's thirst was growing like your man's pikestaff when a colleen is sweet to him. He

found a public house called the Goat and Compasses—
named after the famous gargle-water emporium in
London, obviously—and ordered a pint.

Christ, he thought as the liquor hit his stomach, I
was green and grotty and coming on toward gruesome
for the want of that beer. Even if it was only the weak
brew Americans drank and not to be compared to Guiness's Extra Stout, it was certainly better than a poke
in the eye with a sharp stick.

The pub was almost empty at that hour. Over the
bar was a sign saying NO DOGS OR WOMEN AL-
LOWED. Across from this attempt at sophisticated
wit, on the wall above the window, was a flag with a
coiled snake ready to strike and the motto, DON'T
TREAD ON ME. The side wall had a painting of a
nude female in erotic ecstasy with a swan. The bushes
around them were green as a flag, the woman was
voluptously formed but had orange skin, the swan was
white as a muslin sheet, and the sky a pastel blue that
you only saw on a dandy's weskit; Seamus would wager that the chap who had painted that never heard the
world "garish." The fourth wall had a sign saying NO
GAMBLING OR FOUL LANGUAGE PERMITTED
ON THESE PREMISES AND DON'T TRY TO
STACK THE FUCKING CARDS.

The publican was a red-faced, portly individual
who looked like the sort of fargobawler who would
regard all those decorations as scintillating additions
to the homespun charm of his establishment. He had
probably picked every one of them himself, with great
satisfaction.

A mystery in blue silk European gentleman's clothing sat in a shadowy corner, stirred, translated a glass
from the table to its lips. Clinking *clank* the glass
was returned to the table, and a sun-glint crept

through the window as silently as a burglar to flash sudden gold-purple on the red wine.

A sigh came forth briefly; abrupt, a slight movement followed. "Damnable weather," a human voice, cultured, Continental, ventured from the shadow.

Seamus accepted gladly the implied invitation.

"Sure, the devil himself would be proud to call this town a vestibule of Hell," he said. "But he'd have to turn down the temperature if he wanted to get any fooken work done."

The figure moved forward out of shadow, smiled; Seamus saw a gallant mustache and goatee. Italian skin, eyes that looked deep and missed no more than a collector of bad debts.

"You are from Ireland, a *chara*," the Italian voice drawled.

Seamus was surprised at the Irish phrase; he had never imagined anybody outside Ireland would learn even a smattering of the tongue. He rallied and drawled carelessly, "And you are from Roma, *caro mio*." If he can haul out some Irish, I can remember some *Italiano*. It was strange, though, to think suddenly that *chara* and *caro* were related somehow, and both were cousins of the Latin *caritas* and the English "charity" and "caress."

"Rome is close enough," said the stranger. "Napoli, actually. The world capital of insidious scampi sauces and even more subtle assassins. And you are from Dublin, or is it Bray?"

"A place you probably never heard of," Seamus said. "Dun Laoghaire." *A chara, caro mio, caress,* Seamus was thinking, but what about *charisma* and *cardiac,* and perhaps the *coeur* in *Coeur de Leon* and *courage?*

"The fort of King Laoghaire," the drawl said, also working on etymologies: but the eyes still would not have missed a fly landing on Seamus's ear. "Nine miles south of Dublin. The sea views along there reminded me of Napoli, in fact. Dundalk, Dundrum, Dun Laoghaire—there were once a lot of forts around that part of Dublin Bay."

"You are a world traveler, faith. Nobody ever comes to Dun Laoghaire but English soldiers."

"But your glass is almost empty. Will you permit me?"

And Seamus, with a free beer before him, held out his hand, saying politely, "James Moon," but still wondering privately what sort of Italian would visit a godforsaken place like Dun Laoghaire, and study the Irish language that the Irish themselves hardly spoke anymore.

"Sigismundo ah Malatesta," said the other, taking the hand firmly but briefly. "James Moon would be Seamus Moon back home in Dun Laoghaire?"

So Seamus said "Muadhen" a few times and after "Moo-hen" and "Moo-han" and "Moo'on" and other approximations this chap who wanted to be called Malatesta—Seamus had noted the hesitation about that—miraculously got it right, something no Englishman had ever managed.

"And what were you ever doing in Dun Laoghaire?" Seamus asked finally.

"The same as I am doing here. Writing a little music, tinkering with a few mechanical inventions that never work, and generally avoiding thinking serious thoughts or getting involved in serious issues." Malatesta sipped his wine and stared into the distance. "Perhaps instead of machines, I should invent a devilish new salad dressing. That is the one sure path to immortality in this century.''

And I am not so great a fool as to believe that, Seamus thought. This was a gentleman, certainly, but the drawl and the careful shallowness were all an act, a masque. This chap would buy you a drink out of kindness, but he wouldn't be after giving away any secrets. And those eyes watched like a weasel at a henhouse. Sigismundo "ah Malatesta" had not led the life of the gentry all his days: You could bet a crown on it. But then those Neapolitan blokes had the reputation of being the only boyos in Europe who could swindle a Dutch banker.

"I have no head for mechanical things myself," Seamus said blandly. "And my life has not taught me about salads and such. But I love a good tune."

"And what do you think of this?" Malatesta hummed a few bars, and Seamus sat up sharply. Malatesta hummed a bit more, then stopped. "I lost it there," he said. "I may finish it someday, if a work of art is ever finished. I have a theory that most are just abandoned in despair and given to the public as a bitter private joke. The same may be true of salad dressings, even if chefs seem in general more dedicated men than artists ever are."

The tune had been a variation on *Derry Air,* but more mournful and in some way more hauntingly fragile than the original. It was a child's grief remembered with gentle irony.

"Christ, man, is that yours?"

"No. It is Ireland's. I just added my own exegesis. Neophyte composers borrow, but at my age we steal outright."

"After that," Seamus said firmly, "it is my turn to buy the drinks. Still red wine for you?"

"An incurable Neapolitan habit. Besides, my uncle sells the stuff. I once shot a man because of it, but despite that I still like it."

Maybe this bloke had been drinking longer than Seamus had assumed. He seemed to be what the Irish call a cute man, but a truly cute man wouldn't admit a shooting that casually.

"Are they still looking for you, back in Napoli?" Seamus asked over their new drinks. He made it sound like a casual question.

"Oh, no. It was a duel, and I only wounded the fellow—I didn't kill him. But that was long ago. Nobody remembers it anymore. In Napoli a duel is as easily forgotten as an adultery. To be really infamous you must be overheard to express doubts about Holy Mother Church."

"I almost killed a man once, but a rock fell out of the sky and I got superstitious and lost the belly for it. And I have heard learned men, since then, say that rocks cannot fall out of the sky."

"Nothing is easier than to become a learned man," Malatesta said. "One simply puts one's nose into many books and never raises one's eyes to the world around one. Learned men are almost as tiresome as respectable women."

"You have no regard for scholarship?"

"I respect men whose inventions actually work, as mine never do. And I also respect witty women, all cats of either gender, these strange Virginians who win at cards without cheating—something no Neapolitan ever learned—and any violinist who will follow the score instead of offering an 'interpretation.' "

"And what brings you to América? I came looking for work."

"I came to avoid work. There are those in high

places who want me to do their odd jobs. It is becoming as tedious as Mr. Pope's couplets. I am planning to go to New Orleans and live in a brothel. I have reason to believe that will be beneficial to my music, or my attempt to create an exotic new salad sauce. Since my inventions are by definition eccentric, I regard them as a hobby. Life itself may be a hobby, since it also appears eccentric on close examination.''

After that you can be sure Seamus took a hearty swig of his second beer. "Some can do as they please," he said carefully, "and some need the bloody money so deperately they'll rob and cut throats for it. Is that not a strange world, faith?"

"It is even stranger," said Sigismundo, "that some will rob and kill for money who do not even need money. They already have much. They merely desire to have more. Such men do not listen to music, but only pretend to listen while they plot how to seduce their brothers' wives and embezzle their cousins' assets. Such men rule the world, and what is worse, they do not even employ good cooks."

"Oh, now you're after talking politics. In a backhanded way, bedad."

"Talking politics is as tiresome as reading British novels. I apologize."

"Never in my life have I seen any good come of it."

"Seamus," Sigismundo said kindly. "Seamus Muadhen. You are a wise man."

"Let it go at James Moon. I'm trying to get used to the new language and the new country. And I'm not wise, only wily. We learn that early in Ireland."

"And in Napoli. We have been an occupied country for a long time also. Not as long as Ireland, of course. And we are occupied by the French, who pretend to be logical and are quite mad, while Ireland suffers occupation by the English, which is much more awful since they all pretend to be mad and are coldly logical.''

James Moon—remembering to think of himself that way, in English—drank more golden brown beer with a swift liquid gurgle. "Faith, no place has been occupied as long as Ireland. Do you know what it is, *Signor?* It isn't that we lack brave lads, and I swear before God it isn't that we haven't learned to be foxy and tricky and cute as a shit-house rat—we learned all that four hundred years ago, five hundred years ago, maybe six hundred fooken years ago. Do you know what I'm going to tell you? It's that there is an informer in every pub. He arrives the day they open, with the first barrel of Guiness, and when he dies they replace him. Now what can you do in a country like that?''

Malatesta drank and pondered.

"It is the same in Napoli. My uncle once said that when four conspire in a cellar, three are damned fools and the fourth is a government spy.''

James Moon nodded, with a slight despairing smile almost forming at the corners of his mouth. "Politics is for fools,'' he said wearily.

"They know that in all defeated, conquered countries,'' Sigismundo said, looking into his wine mournfully, as if he suspected it had flies. "I will tell you something stranger. The winners are fools, too, and worse fools than the rebels they hang. You are a perceptive man, I am aware. You can tell I have not led an ordinary life, can you not? Of course you can. It takes a great deal of tragedy to become truly superficial.''

"Must you always talk in oxymorons, man?"

"It is no oxymoron. Those of happy histories can ask what lies behind the surface of things. Those of us who know what lies behind the surface always choose to enjoy every illusion as long as possible. The color of a perfect English rose is in my brain, not in the flower, but I would prefer to enjoy the color than to think dull thoughts like that. Leave philosphy to the innocent. We veterans of infernos and abysses prefer the roses, the sunsets, and beautiful meaningless music."

"Ah, by God, man, you are not sure whether you are a sentimental cynic or a cynical sentamentalist."

"I am sure that it is dangerous to trust in the depths, at sea or on land. Deep men, deep emotions, deep beliefs, deep thoughts, and deep quicksand are all perilous. Give me the superficial and cheerful. The thieves and scoundrels in government I mentioned earlier are merely a nuisance, but a sincere politician can be an international calamity."

"Ah, we are the great pair, the two of us. Sitting here and philosophizing, while the Continental Congress is making more politics according to what I hear."

"It is more dangerous than that," Sigismundo said. "They are probably making history."

"Ah, well, God bless them. I won't be after getting involved myself, but God save them, says I, if they give the English a few bad days."

Sigismundo sipped wine, touched his lips with a napkin, looked strangely at James Moon. "It's not a matter of going out and *getting* involved," he said. "I told you history was worse than politics. You don't go and sign up for it. It comes and gets you. You see, *a chara,* it's the only blood sport in which the inno-cent bystanders are the principal victims.''

He has the Sight, James thought abruptly. That ex-plains his dark humours. Sean O'Lachlann of Meath, who had the Sight, often talked like that, and it was always a warning in disguise. Sometimes the people with the Sight didn't even know at the moment that they were prophesying again. It just comes on them suddenly.

For the first time in three years, he thought of Old Kyte, the town witch in Lousewartshire, who had read the cards for him once, when he worked for the Bab-cocks. His destiny card had been the Hanged Man.

''Ah, Jesus,'' he said, drinking quickly. ''Let us not be getting in the glooms about history and fate and all that, for Christ's sake and for pity's sake and for Jake McCarthy's sake into the bargain. Let us drink up, man.''

And at that moment he heard it, faint at first but then louder and louder in only seconds, like thunder rolling across the sky, like History and Fate and other dark inhuman things coming after a man: a roaring crescendo of *chimes,* first a few bells far away and then hundreds everywhere, hundreds and more hun-dreds, all over Philadelphia, the damned chimes in every church in the city, a pandemonium to knock you off your chair, and then, of course, the howling way up high in the wolf level of not one dog or doz-ens but again hundreds of agonized dogs and hun-dreds of hundreds, all complaining about what the chimes were doing to their sensitive canine ears; and still the chimes were louder than the dogs.

''You see?'' Sigismundo said. ''History is coming to get us. Will you kindly tell them the Italian gen-tleman prefers to play the piano in a brothel? Thank

you, sir. *God save us all from history,"* he growled
suddenly, and then he arose and tipped his hat and
walked out.

I've met my share of strange birds, James Moon
told himself, but this was the strangest yet. The man
regards history as his mortal enemy.

And then he heard the voices in the road, the
shouts, the news passing from street to street.

He drank his beer, left a ha'penny tip, and went
outside, curious but still determined not to get involved. A comfortable job in service, that was all
James Moon wanted in the new land. No politics and
no history: just straight wages, please, a good wife
when he could afford marriage, and a drop of the
creature at evening.

"They've done it! They've done it!" a man was
shouting. "They finally agreed!"

Agreed to what, in the name of God?

But another man was even more eager to spread the
news and he shouted the answer to James's question.

James nodded and went back into the pub. A *declaration of independence*—now what in the world was
that supposed to mean?

"Another pint, your honor," he shouted to the
publican, turning his back on history. The bells were
still ringing and he had to shout.

"It's free," the publican shouted back. "This is a
historical occasion."

"Oh. Ah. Yes." James drank a slow sip. "And
what is this declaration of independence that they
chime bells for? If that's a civil question?"

"We're not British anymore," the publican said
with a broad smile. "We don't pay their God-damned
taxes, and we don't quarter their God-damned sol-

diers, and we don't have to obey their God-damned laws.''

"Oh. Yes. Yes. And won't the British government be after objecting a bit to all that?''

"Let them object. They'll learn better. They can't govern a land this big and this far from London. They'll learn.''

Seamus nodded, wondering how much wishful thinking was in that observation but acting polite. He tried to take another sip. The publican restrained him, and raised a glass he had just poured for himself.

"To liberty,'' he said fiercely.

"To liberty,'' James said, trying to sound sincere. They clinked.

Everybody James had ever heard talking like that had ended up hanging from a tree. He wondered if the Americans were all mad.

Suddenly another man entered the pub. He was about a foot taller than anybody Seamus had ever seen in Ireland or England or in his first month in America. He was a big man from any angle, and Seamus thought in awe, Well, he's not *really* as big as a chestnut tree and probably not as dangerous as the Royal Fusiliers coming at full gallop. But he moved like one who was accustomed to having the world quickly move out of his way, and he had brick-red hair as bright and fiery as James's himself. His clothes were those of a gentlemen, but in the subdued colors the Americans preferred, without the bright, knock-your-eyes-out dyes the English nobility liked to flaunt, but then he didn't really need bright colors. With that hair and that size—around six and a half feet, James guessed—he was about as easy to ignore as a gorilla in a string quartet.

"God *damn* it to hell and breakfast,'' he shouted.

"I need a drink desperately. Publican! Your most devilish whisky—a double shot glass, please—and don't ruin it with water, sir, or I shall have your heart out and *eat* it! I have a gloomy suspicion, amounting almost to a terrible certainty, that the crazy bastards in the Continental Congress will no longer be satisfied at my holding the lobsterbacks at bay, but will want me and my poxy troops to drive them from the North American continent, Jesus H. particular Christ and his black bastard brother Rastus, what have I done to deserve that?"

And that was how James Moon met his great and good friend, George Washington, and that was the ultimate reason why James's great-great-great-great-great-great-great-great-grandson was tear-gassed by the Chicago police in Lincoln park in the year 1968 along with William S. Burroughs, the lead singer from a rock group called the Fugs, a lot of clergymen, journalists from several nations, a *Playboy* editor, and the nephew of the great-great-great-great-great-great-great-granddaughter of the Italian who had left the pub so quickly when he heard history approaching in the distance.

The three assassins who came looking for the Italian a month later thought they were lucky when the publican remembered an Italian gentleman who hated politics and was headed for New Orleans. They embarked for New Orleans quickly, convinced that they were closing in.

4. A Reverser of Laws

Infinity—Southern Ohio 1776

Truth is an arrow with two points

Returning, as always, he had the problem of becoming again a human being, in a human body, in one specific place, and adjusting again to the limits that a body and a place implied. Only then was he ready for the effort of forgetting—forcing himself to forget—the knowledge of his own infinity.

I am here, on this soil, beneath this maple tree. I hear the sound of the water rushing in the creek. I smell the rich grassy earth smell. I am not an infinite star in infinite space. I am a limited human being with a limited human personality.

Miskasquamish. That was his name here, his name in the Maheema tribe. His real name, as always, must be secret.

Yes, he reminded himself, it must be secret especially from the bear-people. He had to remember continually that the bear-people could do terrible magic if they ever learned his real name. It was bad enough that they knew his tribal name.

Now he was fully back, the world was solid and fragrant and green around him, and he knew what he had to do. He had to find the dangerous one, the Reverser of Laws, enemy of the Wakan, enemy of the

Maheema tribe, enemy of all humans and the star people.

The one called Sackymondo.

Miskasquamish had been a man of medicine for more moons than most men ever see. He had smoked all the magic herbs and gone on voyages to all the magic realms. He could heal those who needed healing and he could kill those who needed killing.

He knew that the people of the Maheema tribe respected him, almost to the point of fearing him, but that was because they did not understand that each of them was like him. They dreamed one world because that was their habit. All worlds were open to them, as they were to him, but they were afraid to walk through the gates.

The fools thought he had walked through the gate willingly. Like all men of medicine, he knew the truth: the gate suddenly opened and pulled you in. You had no choice in the matter. Nor was there any logic in who it picked for the voyage.

The tribe remembered when he had the Evil Talk sickness, of course, and they had worried about him then, almost two hundred moons ago. They worried because the Maheema knew, all the tribes knew, that a man with the Evil Talk sickness never becomes normal again. It is the great curse and the great blessing of the Evil Talk, that none who have it return to full humanity again. They either become men of medicine, like Miskasquamish, or they become the enemies of men and gods, the Reversers of Laws. That was because truth is an arrow with two points: It includes opposites where ordinary men and women exclude opposites.

Because the truth points in two directions, Miskasquamish was more like the Reversers of Laws than the tribe realized. He knew the Evil Talk, and he knew the Reversers of Laws, because they were the opposite points of his own will. That was why he could understand the Reversers of Laws and they could sometimes understand him.

Like a man of medicine, a Reverser of Laws knows the infinity within. He knows the Wakan, the One Inside All Things. A Reverser of Laws is free and drunk in his freedom and he is so irresponsible that he might even do good things occasionally because he is not even consistent in his deviltry.

And now the Maheema people were threatened by a new Reverser of Laws, one who was invisible and not yet apparent to them. Only Miskasquamish knew that there was a Reverser of Laws in the land.

It had begun half a moon ago when the blue-crested bird sang a new song. The tribe marveled and asked Miskasquamish what it meant, that a bird should sing a new song, and he had lied to them, as men of medicine must often lie, because ordinary people will go mad if they hear too much truth at once. Miskasquamish said the bird sang a new song because there would be good hunting this winter.

A man of medicine can look straight at a Sky Demon, He who Walks on the Wind, and not show his fear.

Miskasquamish knew that the blue-crested bird had been singing his own secret name, which only he himself knew, and the Wakan inside all things. It was the Wakan singing through the bird and it was a warning.

When he was alone, then, he had smoked the five herbs of the morning star and the herb of the Moon Lady, and he had gone to the dream mountain and talked to the Lady who knows all secrets and they had wept together and he had come back to be brave and to hide from the tribe the terrible truth.

Every day then he would smoke a special herb and scan.

The Reverser of Laws did not come closer, but he did not go away either.

Miskasquamish cut his arm in a long swift gash and drank the blood and smoked the mushroom of the sky-walkers and went to the star-people and they were afraid and would not help him.

The Reverser of Laws was still nearby.

The Moon Lady could not help. The star-people were frightened. The tribe would go mad if they knew. There was no choice then. You do not go to the gate, ever. The gate opens and pulls you in. Miskasquamish went in search of the Reverser of Laws.

He knew the right direction, and after the first day he knew the name—a strange name, neither Maheema nor Ojibway nor any tribe of these times. Siggy Moondo Chilline. Or Sigs Monday. Or Sackymondo. Something foreign, alien, not even in the tongue of the star-people.

After the second day, Miskasquamish could see the Reverser of Laws but still did not know how far away he was. A white man, like those reported near the Father of Waters by the Chickasaw people, but not perfectly white, almost bronze, and not blonde of hair or blue in the eyes. Black of hair and eye, like a Maheema: very black. Hair growing on his chin, and more hair around his mouth. Not living in an ordinary tipi but in a strange, new kind of tipi made of logs and with square corners.

The third day was terrible. If Miskasquamish were a singer of songs instead of a man of medicine, he would have written a ballad about it for the tribe. It was a mighty conflict with the bear-people, two of them together, and they recognized him at once. All the bear-people knew Miskasquamish and hated him, because of the magic he had done to keep them out of Maheema territory. He had to run very fast, but a man of so many moons could not run fast enough to escape the bear-people, and they almost caught him. He had to do very much magic to blind them and paralyze them for the time it took him to escape and hide.

On the fourth day, Miskasquamish found the Reverser of Laws.

There was a clearing in the woods, and in the middle of it, as Miskasquamish had seen in a dream, was a square tipi made out of logs. It had square holes in the walls and clear magic crystals in the squares that let light pass inward to the tipi. All as seen in advance.

The Reverser of Laws was sitting under a tree, very still. For a moment, Miskasquamish thought the man's spirit was away with the star-people and only his body sat there: He was that quiet. But then he looked up and spoke.

"You look exactly as I expected," he said. "I've been seeing you in dreams for over ten years now."

Miskasquamish made the peace sign, hiding his fears and summoning bravery within him.

If Sikymundo had learned to speak Maheema, that proved he was the most dangerous kind of Reverser of Laws. White men (everybody knew this) never learned Indian languages. They insisted that the Indians must learn their languages.

This will be a long struggle and I may not win, Miskasquamish thought.

"I have seen you in my dreams, also," he said noncommittally.

The Reverser arose and went into his strange square tipi.

Miskasquamish waited. He did not try any magic, and he did not consider running away. The gate had opened and this was his latest challenge.

The Reverser came out of the tipi with furs.

"For you," he said.

Miskasquamish took the furs. He thought very quickly then, and removed a strong medicine pouch from his belt. It would not do to fake and hand over a weak pouch.

"For you," he said.

The Reverser accepted the pouch.

They both sat down. The Reverser, even if he was a white man, knew how to be polite. He did not stare, he did not fidget, and he did not rush.

The two of them, Miskasquamish and Sigamoondo, looked at the bushes and trees and listened to bird songs. In the distance was the bubbling sound of the yellow brook with the fiery earth spirit in it.

"I mean no harm to the Maheema people," Sigamoondo said.

Reversers would say things like that. Sometimes they believed it.

"Those are handsome furs," Miskasquamish said. "You are rich and generous."

"This pouch is strong medicine. I can feel it. You are a man of wisdom and power."

They waited again. Miskasquamish admitted to himself that this one had good manners for a Reverser.

Miskasquamish made a formal speech then.

"The trees," he said, "follow the laws of trees. The racoon-people follow the laws of racoons. The moon follows her laws. The bubbling brook that we hear now follows the laws of the brooks and rivers. It is old knowledge that all things under the sky have each their own laws. It is good that the world is so.'' He did not make the accusation explicit.

The Reverser went to a hole in the ground that had a rope on a turner above it. He pulled down on one end of the rope and by some Reverser magic the other end came up with a bucket having water in it.

Miskasquamish kept his face immobile, even though he had never seen this kind of magic before, even from a Reverser.

The Reverser drank first to be polite. Whatever magic the water from the bucket had was not dangerous to him, Miskasquamish realized.

''Have some.''

Miskasquamish kept his face impassive and drank, wondering what would happen.

The Reverser sat beside him again.

''The laws of the trees are not the laws of the beaver-people,'' he said. ''The laws of the Maheema are not the laws of the Chickasaw. The laws of the brooks are not the laws of the stars.''

The magic water still had no more effect than ordinary water.

''All things have different laws,'' Miskasquamish said. ''That is true. But all things are bound by law nonetheless. Except for the Reversers.''

''All who are not ordinary people are not men of medicine,'' the Reverser said. ''All who are not men of medicine are not Reversers.''

Miskasquamish arose. ''I thank you for the furs,'' he said.

''I thank you for the medicine pouch.''

''It is possible we may meet again.''

''It is.''

Miskasquamish walked away carefully, not looking back and not hurrying.

The Reverser claimed he was not a Reverser, but that was what you would expect. Reversers reverse everything.

Thirty yards from the clearing, Miskasquamish heard the sound behind him. It was not like the brook or the river in flood, not like thunder and not like the wildcat howling in heat, not like the tom-tom and not like a medicine chant. Miskasquamish had never heard such sound before. It could almost be called beautiful, except that it was so strange: a kind of sound that Miskasquamish had never imagined.

The Reverser had gone into his tipi and was making his own reverse kind of music.

Miskasquamish spent two days hunting before he was ready to return.

When he entered the clearing, the Reverser was sitting under the tree like a dead man again, but he was watching. Those eyes never stopped watching, Miskasquamish thought uneasily.

Miskasquamish walked over to the Reverser and laid his furs—twice as many as he had received—on the ground.

"For you," he said. Then he sat.

The Reverser took a bag from his belt and laid it before Miskasquamish. "For you."

They looked at the trees and listened to the yellow healing brook.

Miskasquamish opened the bag finally. Wonderful magic stones and crystals of incredible beauty. He understood at once. Just as he had brought twice as many furs as he had received, the Reverser was giving twice as much magic as he had been given.

They looked at the trees awhile, once again.

Miskasquamish filled a pipe. He used only two magic herbs, not wanting to raise the contest to a higher level. If the Reverser made the water come up from the ground in a bucket again, it might be demon water the second time.

They shared the pipe.

"Once," Miskasquamish said, "I had the Evil Talk sickness. All men and women feared me. The gate that is not a gate had opened, and I was afraid. I was not able to confront it as a man. I became a boy again, a cowardly boy. I am still ashamed. Finally, I passed through the gate. It was not terrible on the other side. Only going through the gate is terrible."

Siggymundo smoked some more, then passed the pipe back courteously.

"The son of my father's brother had the Evil Talk sickness," he said. "He did not pass through the gate. He jumped in a great water, a water bigger than a river, because he was so afraid."

"The grandfather of my uncle's pet possum was once fucked by a green and blue moose," Miskasquamish said, not hiding his anger this time.

"Very well," the Reverser said, wearily accepting the rebuke. "Antonio, the boy I mentioned, was not the only one in our family to have the Evil Talk sickness. You know I had it just as I know you had it."

Miskasquamish pretended forgiveness. "Why did you not speak straight the first time?" he asked as if in sympathy.

"In my tribe we do not speak straight the first time."

Miskasquamish waited.

"There are many men of medicine where I come from," Siggymoondo said. "You would not know their

names. Some are Free Builders and some are Black
Stone Men and some are Red Earth Men, as close as
I can call them in your speech. They all have different
medicine, and they all fear me as you do, even though
I mean no harm to anyone.''

Miskasquamish rose. "These are beautiful crystals,'' he said.

"These are beautiful furs.''

"We may meet again.''

"We may.''

Miskasquamish walked away, as before, not looking
back. He was furious, but a man of medicine does not
act rashly.

The Reverser had told him, insolently, while pretending to be polite as they all do, that many men of
medicine had tried to stop his evil progress and all had
failed. He had lied again, still pretending he meant no
harm. He had come here to work his evil on the Maheema, because there were no challenges left where
he came from.

A Reverser, like a man of medicine, has been to the
Wakan, the One Inside All Things, and has learned
that he himself is not different from the Wakan. But a
man of medicine is still a man, loyal to his tribe. A
Reverser has become like the Wakan, inhuman, not
loyal to any tribe, not loyal to any spirits or gods.
Because he is like the Wakan, he thinks he can play
with the world and all the worlds.

And this Reverser would be harder to kill than any
of the others.

5. The Light Sings Eternal

Brandywine 1777

Once we were all stars

"**P**rivate Moon of A Company, sir. I have a dispatch for you, sir."

General Washington looked up vaguely, like a mathematician interrupted in the middle of a quadratic equation. "Oh?" he said. "More bad news, I assume." He didn't seem to recognize James at all, even though he had recruited him into the Continental Army.

"The situation is no better, sir," James said carefully. He would rather leave the tent before Washington read of the latest Hessian victory.

"Well, that's war," the general said cheerfully. He was as worried looking as a locked safe. "You win some and you lose some." He beamed, nodding his head philosophically.

When are you ever going to win some, James thought. It wasn't wise to say that. "Do you accept the dispatch, sir?"

The General toked at his pipe, deeply and thoughtfully. James felt dizzy from the fumes already in the cramped tent.

"Oh, I accept the dispatch, Private." The general

suddenly seemed to focus and recognize James Moon. ''I accept the ineluctable, James. That is the path of philosophy, is it not?''

James was stunned. Generals were never this casual with privates, and General Washington in particular was a man of stern adherence to military hierarchy. ''You express it very well, sir,'' he said. That, at least, was safe.

''Have you ever observed,'' the general asked, ''that under proper conditions of sunlight, a single drop of dew on the point of a blade of grass will contain all the colors of the *rainbow?* It is most admirable and gives one to wonder at the glory of the Creator.''

There was a long pause. James could not leave until the general dismissed him, but the general seemed to have forgotten that he was there.

The fumes were getting thicker and James felt a little drunk and strangely elated. Faith, what ferocious tobacco were the Indians after selling the general lately? Only in January, he had insisted on having all the troops *stuck with needles*—in the arms, it was, and it hurt like bloody hell—because some quack doctor in France claimed that would prevent further spread of the smallpox. The general was *weird* at times, James thought uneasily.

''And is it not strange,'' the general went on, toking and philosophizing, ''that we conventionally believe the rainbow to have seven colors, whereas a close examination of the spectrum, in a dew drop such as I mentioned, reveals an infinity of subtle and most gorgeous gradations of hue? I have been thinking deeply about this recently and am astounded that we normally notice so *little* of nature's glorious raiment.''

''Um, yes. Sir.''

This gentle absentminded man was not the Wash-

ington that James had learned to know in the year he
had served under him. The Washington James knew
was withdrawn, yes, but never relaxed or reflective.
He was also the most foul-mouthed man James had
met since leaving Dublin County and could curse for
two hours without repeating himself when a junior officer disappointed him. Only yesterday James had
heard him in typical form, correcting a lieutenant who
had erred: "By hatchet heads and hammer handles and
the howling harlots of Hell, you are the most *incompetent idiot* I have ever encountered, sir! You are lower
than a snake's cunt, sir! If my dog had a face like
yours, sir, hanged if I wouldn't shave his arse and teach
him to walk backwards!" That was the George Washington that James knew. That was the man who had
maintained discipline through a whole year of defeats
and desperate retreats.

"Um, ah, sir?"

"Are you a mystic, James?"

"Well, sir, they do be saying that all Irishmen are
mystics. I once saw a rock fall out of the sky."

"A rock fall out of the sky?" The general put down
his pipe and stared. "I have seen strange things but
never a *rock* falling out of the sky. Were you sober at
the time?"

"As God is my witness, sir."

"Only ignorant peasants say rocks fall out of the
sky, James. Learned men say it is impossible."

"Yes, sir, but I saw it, sir."

"You swear you saw it, when I tell you learned men
say it is impossible?"

"I saw what I saw, sir."

The General smiled secretively. "You are excused,
private."

The next day James discovered that he had been promoted to colonel, and died, and went to heaven, but got thrown out because there were two of him.

The battle of Brandywine is not much remembered in America, but in France they know all about it because the Marquis de Lafayette was wounded there. In County Clare, Ireland—especially in the Burren—they know all about it because Colonel Seamus Muadhen saw God there, sort of, and discovered that God was Irish.

Seamus told that story many times after he returned to Ireland and lived in the Burren. He told how he had met General Washington in a pub in Philadelphia and leaped at the chance to fight the Brits. He never mentioned that Washington had gotten him blind drunk before he made that patriotic decision, and that, while sober, he had been firmly convinced he wanted no part of any war anywhere at any time for any cause.

Nor did he talk to the men of the Burren about his knowledge that he would fight another war soon, this time for Ireland.

At Brandywine in 1777, Colonel Muadhen—or Colonel Moon, as he was then calling himself—was shot right off of his horse by a Hessian bullet. He had only one thought as he fell: *Bejesus, but my career as an officer has been a bloody short one.* He was quite convinced he was dying—a man hit by a bullet that knocks him off his horse doesn't have time to wonder where he was wounded. He simply assumes the matter is very serious.

He never hit the ground. Instead, he made a sharp turn in midair, rose rapidly, and found himself looking down at the battlefield.

Oh, good Christ, I'm on my way to heaven, he thought.

A singing light approached rapidly, covered him in a glory of golden love, bathed him in motherly kindness. It was better than sexual orgasm: He felt himself literally bursting like a broken glass and yet also blooming slowly like a flower.

He came apart into two stars.

—*Oh, you damned eejit, look what you went and got yourself into now,* Seamus Muadhen said.

—*You aren't real,* James Moon answered. *I must be having a fever. I am a wounded man and you mustn't bedevil me. I think I was hit in the leg and the doctors may be after sawing it off on me.*

—*This is no fever, and you are no James Moon. You are me, and I am you.*

—*A name is only a name. There aren't really two of us just because I have two names. This is all a hallucination. I have been shot and this is a fever.*

—*Then why are you answering me?*

James looked down. Men with a stretcher were carrying his body back to the field hospital. He could see blood gushing from his, or the body's, right leg.

—*Oh, be damned to it, there are* three *of us. You and me and the body down there on earth. This war has been a fair bugger for a year and now it has driven me mad entirely.*

—*Never mind that. It is time you and I had an understanding. You have been keeping me in an underground jail of your mind too long.*

—*And what kind of talk is that? In jail, is it? You are only a name, not a person.*

—*I am a person as much as you are, James. More than you, bedad. I am the true man, and you are only the masque. The shadow of the man.*

—*Talk sense, man. You sound like you've been drinking the poteen.*

—*Every Irishman has two selves, James. His true self and the masque he learns to wear in dealing with the conquerors, the* sasanach. *You have become the masque and lost the true self. Once we were all stars and we've been after making Punch and Judy puppets of ourselves.*

—*And I would be a great fool to believe such madness. You have a few jars on you, I swear. It is I who am the real man and you who are the puppet of my hallucination.*

—*That is the great lie of the conquerors. Sure they have been after putting a bloody brutal scissors to our souls, in Ireland, and cutting out all that is Irish in us. They want us to be imitation Englishmen. And what is* James Moon *if not an imitation Englishman?*

—*I will listen to no more of such talk from the likes of you, phantom that you are. I am dying in a war against England and you are but a symptom of my fever, I still say. To your face I say it.*

—*Peter denied Christ three times. How many times will you deny me?*

—*Don't be comparing yourself to God, now. That's too blasphemous even for a goblin like yourself.*

—*But I am God, James—very God of very God. The True Self of every living being is the one God. And you great fools, who are only masques and shadows of men, are always after denying the starry Christ within, Pontius Pilates and Peters that you are.*

—*Ow. Be careful there. That hurt like bloody hell, it did.*

—*Be calm, sir. We are taking out the bullet. You will live.*

And Seamus Muadhen was gone and there was a medical officer looking down at James, because James was suddenly back in his body again, and now he felt all the pain at once.

But at least he was alive.

Or was he? It seemed, after the operation, that James Moon was dead. They did not have to saw off his leg— the bullet came out quickly, without the blood poison setting in—but somebody had sawed off his identity.

Colonel Seamus Muadhen—he insisted on being called that, now—recuperated slowly in a hospital near Brandywine. The man in the next bed was a French marquis, Major General de Lafayette, and he and Seamus had a great deal to talk about, because each of them was convinced he was a little bit off his head. Seamus thought he had bats in his belfry because he wasn't sure how much to believe of his trip halfway to heaven, or how James Moon had died and left himself alive, remembering that he once was a star. The marquis thought he had had owls in his attic because the staff of the hospital did not talk like ordinary Americans or even like ordinary English people.

The staff of the hospital all talked like characters out of Shakespeare.

The marquis worried about this a great deal at first. He worried that he was really in an English hospital and they were all talking that way to drive him mad, or to make him think he was mad, to punish him for volunteering to fight for the rebels. He worried that such an extravagant theory indicated that he really was mad. He worried that they weren't talking that way at all and he was simply hallucinating all the time.

"And how is thee today?" said a nurse coming to his bedside.

"I am much improved," the marquis said, controlling his anxiety. "And how is, ah, um, *thee?*"

"The Good Lord has been good to this humble servant. But do thee need anything to read? More blankets, perhaps? We wish thee to be comfortable here.''

That was the way it was every time he talked to one of them. The marquis finally got up the courage to discuss it with Colonel Muadhen, the Irish officer who was raving about having two souls when they brought him in.

"The mental effects of a wound can be longer lasting than the physical effects," Major General Lafayette said carefully.

"Oh, aye. I'm not a-fevered anymore, but I still wonder about those two souls a bit."

"It wears off in time, I suppose, or all old soldiers would be mad."

"That is a cheerful way to be looking at it."

"I've had my own problem, to be frank."

"That I was sure of. You have had a most absent and heartsore expression at times."

"The truth is," the marquis said, "everybody here sounds, well, strange." He took a breath. "They sound like Shakespeare without the poetry."

Seamus laughed, and then looked sympathetic. "Oh, bejesus, Shakespeare is it? You've never read the King James Bible, I gather?"

"What are you trying to tell me?" The Major General had picked up all his English in a six-month crash course after deciding to join the American Revolution. The young and unsure King Louis XVI—"the fat boy," Lafayette called him—had forbidden this madcap project, so technically the marquis was in the colonies illegally and subject to arrest if he returned to France.

"It is not Shakespeare they are after imitating," Colonel Muadhen explained. "It is the English Bible. It is part of their religion to talk as well as act like our

Lord, and they imagine he talked like their Bible. I haven't the heart to tell them he probably spoke Hebrew.''

After that the marquis recovered much faster, but he spent most of his time talking to the hospital staff and learning all he could about them and their strange religion. Why did they think God disapproved of bright, happy-looking colors on clothing and wanted them to wear black all the time? Because God wished men to work out their salvation in fear and trembling, they said. Why did they think God disapproved of slavery? Because he made all souls in his own image. If they would not take their hats off for the king, and would nurse soldiers wounded fighting the king, why did they think fighting the king was still a sin anyway? Because he said, *Thou shalt not kill.* Would they fight even if a ruffian were trying to rob their goods or murder their families? No, because on the Cross, Christ said, *Father, forgive them.*

The Marquis de Lafayette found the Quakers of Brandywine almost as astounding and wonderful as Voltaire's story about the visitor from Sirius who walks across the earth and never notices the human race crawling around beneath his toes. He had never before met Christians who didn't hate one another and he found it extraordinary.

He was only mildly disillusioned when he heard one male nurse, in a discussion of whose turn it was to empty the bedpans, tell another, ''Oh, go fuck thyself.''

General Washington found time to visit the Quaker hospital, despite the distraction of supervising yet another retreat. He sat by Major General Lafayette's bed and talked, gravely and with great sincerity, about the debt America owned the marquis, who had shed his blood in the cause of a nation not his own, and he said that the United States would never forget what it owned to the de Lafayette family of France.

Seamus discovered that Washington, like himself, seemed to be three men. The man who spoke of national gratitude to Lafayette was not the roaring effing-and-blinding disciplinarian Seamus had seen most often, nor was he the absentminded philosopher of twelve days ago in the tent. He was a statesman, and he knew how to use unction.

Later, while Seamus was walking in the garden—he had gone out to allow Washington and Lafayette some privacy—a giant shadow fell between him and the sun. There was only one man in Seamus's experience who could cast a shadow that huge.

"Good afternoon, General."

"Good afternoon, Colonel."

They walked a few paces. Today Washington did not seem to have the peculiar lurching gait that had afflicted him in recent months. An American robin circled above their heads, landed in a tree, and loudly announced that he could lick any bird in the garden with one wing tied behind him.

"You saw a rock fall from the sky," Washington said. "And you believed your own eyes, instead of popular opinion."

"I did that, General." Seamus was not going to pour out his heart about his other soul, the one that was a star. The falling rock business was queer enough.

The robin announced shrilly that he was half-horse and half-alligator, ate falcons for breakfast, and would hold this territory until the magpies learned to dance the pavanne and hell froze over. European robins, Seamus thought, were more tactful. Across the garden, a crow laughed derisively and muttered a few animad-versions about upstart braggarts in borrowed feathers.

"Well, then go shit in thy hat," a medical orderly shouted in the kitchen. "And clap it on thy head for curls."

"I saw something stranger than a falling rock from heaven once," Washington said. "I was working as a surveyor for the colonial government. I was alone in the woods for months and months. You get a bit, ah, fanciful sometimes when you are alone too long. But I saw something more remarkable than your falling rock, and I believed it."

"I understand, General. You decided to trust yourself instead of popular notions of what's real and what's unreal."

A butterfly fluttered by. And Madam I'm Adam, Seamus thought, waiting.

"Yes," Washington said.

The robin announced that he was moving to a more salubrious climate and flew off. The crow raucously told him not to hurry his return.

"You wouldn't care to talk about it, General?" Seamus asked softly.

"You should probably think me mad. But this event is why you are a Colonel today."

"Because I trusted myself instead of popular opinions. Is that what you mean, General?"

"That is what I mean, Colonel. Go on trusting yourself. We must meet and talk on other occasions."

General Washington walked off, aloof, gigantic, enigmatic again. Until Polyphemus escapes from the *Odyssey* and comes knocking at my door, Seamus thought, that man will serve as the most desperate character I ever encountered.

It was not until three years later that General Washington finally told Colonel Muadhen about the star that came out of the sky, that night long ago in the woods, and the Italian Arab or Arabian Italian who got out of the star and spoke to him, and prophesied his future in accurate detail.

The Italian or Arab who rode in the star had said, at the end, "Never fear, never doubt, never despair. We shall raise you higher than the kings of Europe."

Then the Arab or Italian repeated formally, "We met on the square, we part on the level," and climbed back into the star. He made some mechanical adjustments, leaned out the window, and shouted, "Remember, now—no wife, no horse, no mustache!" and flew straight up in the air and away over the treetops at an angle of thirty-three degrees like a shot of shit off a shovel.

6. The Marquis de Sade and Other Libertines

England–France–America 1776–1986

The Wonderful and all-important Willy so crucial to the Christian definition of Holiness

SUBVERSIVE DOCUMENT GAINS WIDE READERSHIP; HANCOCK INSOLENT

Even before 1776 was over, the Declaration of Independence composed by Mr. Tom Jefferson, Gent., of Charlottesville, Virginia (b. 1743, attorney, planter, architect), was officially published at 48 High Street in Philadelphia and the world was informed in silver-plate prose that certain liberal, libertarian, and down-right libertine propositions derivative or deducible from the philosophy of John Locke (1632–1704, auth. "Essay Concerning Human Understanding," "Letter on Toleration," "Two Treatises of Civil Government") were "self-evident," even though the governments of the civilized world had been acting on directly opposed propositions for about forty-five hundred years.

A large part of the literate world read Mr. Jefferson's political treatise and was, according to temperment, astounded, elated, or agitated. Everybody in Europe heard the story of how Mr. John Hancock (b. 1737, smuggler) of Massachusetts Bay signed the Declaration first, in large letters, saying, "There, I guess King George will be able to read that!"—a remark that was regarded as uncouth in genteel circles and contributed much to the American reputation for barbarism, unruliness, and lack of respect for authority.

FOUL LANGUAGE USED BY REBEL LEADER; SENSIBILITIES SHOCKED

A new and larger Continental Army was raised, with Mr. Geo. Washington (b. 1732, planter and gentleman of Virginia), as its leader, and a lottery was held to raise funds to pay the soldiers *something,* if they survived the smallpox that had been decimating their ranks for months.

The pestilence was everywhere, north and south, in the cities as well as in the army. So far in 1776, it had killed over half the soldiers in the Continental Army, reducing Washington's recruits from over ten thousand to only about five thousand. With the remnant and some exhilarating herbs in his pipe, he set off to challenge the largest Empire in the history of the planet, and, of course, the still pox-ridden and largely ill-nourished troops were soundly trounced on every possible occasion, despite Washington's vehement exhortations to his officers that he would eat thunderclouds and ball lightning and breathe hellfire, sulphur and damnation and by Jesus and Mary Christ, sirs, kick their useless arses to kingdom come and back if they did not do better. Such abusive and intemperate language was recorded on several occasions and ladies of refinement were known to swoon in horror when the revolutionary firebrand was quoted verbatim in cultured drawing rooms.

HOWE CONCILATORY,
ADAMS INTRANSIGENT,
FRANKLIN'S MODERATION UNHEEDED

By September, General Howe was sure the Colonies would come to their senses soon. He arranged a secret meeting on Staten Island with the famous Dr. Benjamin Franklin (b. 1706, printer, aphorist, mechanical/electrical inventor, peregrinator) and two Congressmen named Rutledge and Adams. A Whig and a sympathizer with the just complaints of the Colonists, Howe was prepared to negotiate reasonably. The insolent, intransigent, and intolerable Adams bluntly informed him there was one nonnegotiable demand: The Crown *must* recognize the independence of the Colonies. Howe departed in despair, but he remembered the name of the man who would not negotiate reasonably: John Adams, by God, of Braintree, in Massachusetts Bay, by God. An absolute raving lunatic, by God. The kind of man, by God, who would absolutely come to his end on a gallows some day, by God.

PAST DEEDS OF BRAINTREE BARRISTER
RECALLED

General Howe was not cognizant that the Continental Congress had had the same opinion of Adams (b. 1735, farmer, attorney, essayist) when he first started agitating them for Independence. Nor did Howe know that, after a few months, Congress had all agreed Mr. Adams of Braintree was not only mad but rude, conceited, and sarcastic. Howe was not apprised of the fact that the irascible Adams had gone on, despite that,

to argue and marshall logic and rhetoric, and wit, and
learning, and satire, and facts, and figures, and selected judicious quotes from Lord Coke's judiciously
selected *Institutes,* and redundance, and repetition,
and total sincerity, and a complete lack of charisma
and political grace until, by some magic, he persuaded
them to appoint Mr. Jefferson to write a Declaration
of Independence, and then induced them to sign the
treasonous and libertine document. Howe did not
know that five years ago Adams had, by similar sincerity and lack of political realism—and at a time when
defending "Lobsterbacks" was like wearing a leper's
bell (the pejorative term "Lobsterbacks" being that
insult applied to His Majesty's troops by the Colonists
in Massachusetts)—marvelously and wonderfully persuaded a Boston jury to acquit Captain Preston, a British officer who had fired on an American mob who
were stoning his men. Adams had won, then, because
he sincerely believed Captain Preston had acted in self-
defense and that the cause of the Colonies must not
depart one jot from pure Justice as he understood it.
As in Philadelphia, once Adams was convinced he
was right, he argued until everybody else thought he was
right, too.

MUSICAL NOTES FROM OLD VIENNA—AND
AN IMPORTANT INVENTION REPORTED

Wolfgang Amadeo (a.k.a. Amadeus) Mozart (b.
1756, composer, performer, seducer) produced his
lyrically sweet Haffner Serenade and his more stark
and resonant *Serenata Notturna* in Vienna that year,
whilst in Elmsford, New York, a barmaid named Betsy
Flannagan invented the cocktail. All three productions
added much to the subsequent amusement and be-

musement of the world, but did little to improve the dark humour of Seamus Muadhen, who had gotten decidedly inebriated with General Washington in the quaint old Philadelphia tavern styled The Goat and Compasses (a derivative of the similar establishment in London Town, misnamed by an imperfectly educated sign painter who had been commissioned to engrave the religious message, "God encompasseth") and woke up with that vile distemper called the "hangover" in vulgar speech and also discovered to his consternation that he had enlisted in the most pox-ridden army in the most hopeless war in the history of human optimism and folly.

ADAM S. AND ADAM W.—A DYNAMIC DUO STRIKES, FEUDALISM REELS

Before 1776 was over, Adam Smith quietly published *The Wealth of Nations* in Scotland and Adam Weishaupt, even more quietly, founded the Order of the Illuminati in Bavaria, which quickly infiltrated Freemasonic lodges throughout Europe and even in the American colonies; the Illuminati also established a branch at Harvard University, called Phi Betta Kappa, as you may read in Heckethorn's erudite and exhaustive *The Secret Societies of All Ages and Countries*. In England, Sir John Babcock and David Hartley and a few other radicals tried to persuade Parliament to abolish slavery entirely, importation of new slaves having been prohibited since 1772. But for a large part of the English reading public all these events were overshadowed by the Lady Maria Babcock scandal and the subsequent and bloodcurdling Beckersniff blasphemies.

John Wilkes, the demagogue, rogue, and erstwhile

convict who boldly supported the Americans in Parliament, was also heard to support both Lady Babcock and the obscene Beckersniff woman. "By Gad, sir," he said to all and sundry, "these are two wenches *with balls!*"

Evidently Mr. Wilkes meant the remark as a compliment.

NEAPOLITAN MUSICIAN SEEKS REST AND SOLITUDE

Sigismundo Celine (b. 1750, sun in Capricorn, moon in Leo, Gemini rising) sat under a tree, meditating.

All phenomena, to him, were equally real, equally unreal, equally inexplicable, equally marvelous.

After escaping from the religious maniacs who wanted to make him Emperor of Europe, Sigismundo had eventually run as far as southern Ohio to be sure they would not find him again. Traveling around Europe, originally, he had used the name Sigismundo Malatesta and let it be thought he was a painter. In the American colonies, he had admitted he was a musician—worried that he might be leaving a Clue for his pursuers (if he still had pursuers)—but then bedeviled his trail by telling everybody to whom he spoke that he planned to go to New Orleans.

After arriving in Ohio, he had seen no human being for a period that, in his isolation, seemed almost eternal to him. That suited him perfectly. The work in building a log cabin was both exhausting and exhilarating, as he had hoped. He meditated for longer and longer periods every day, using the techniques the Priory had taught him in Egypt, emptying his mind of its acquired characteristics until it was like a mirror—void, shining, reflecting a universe that was real and unreal and inexplicable and marvelous all at once.

BEYOND GOOD AND EVIL

In this real, unreal, inexplicable, marvelous mirror there had been recurrent phenomena or epiphenomena involving a crazy old sorcerer who thought Sigismundo was a Reverser—which seemed to be the most evil kind of Black Magician—because Sigismundo regarded all phenomena as equally real and equally unreal and did not distinguish ''right'' and ''wrong.'' To be in that amoral prehuman state was to be a monster, the sorcerer seemed to believe.

Sigismundo was not sure he believed in any classic or philosophical external objectivity (in an Aristotelian sense) of the crazy old sorcerer. He had once had equally realistic dialogues with Uncle Pietro when he was alone in a dungeon, while being held prisoner by the *other* gang of religious maniacs who had dogged him all his life, the ones who wanted to make sure he never became Emperor of Europe.

It didn't matter whether he believed in Miskasqamic or not. The old sorcerer was another phenomenon and all phenomena were equally true, equally false, and equally meaningless.

Sigismundo intended to meditate, with or without the phenomena and/or epiphenomena of Miskasqamic, until he died—or until he decided to get involved with the damned race of two-legged idiots and devils who called themselves humans again, if that ever happened.

Sigismundo had come to the deep Ohio woods seeking the solititude to make his mind an empty mirror

at the age of twenty-six. That was the result of being
involved with conspirators and magicians since he was
fourteen.

MIGRATION OF LOYAL CITIZENS TO NEUTRAL ZONE

By autumn 1777, Seamus Muadhen was a Colonel (because of the rock that fell out of the sky), a hero (because
of the wound at Brandywine), and a patriot (because of
his Celtic adoration of words utilized with precise ele-
gance). He had read the Declaration of Independence and
was convinced Mr. Jefferson must be an Irishman, because he wrote better English than the English ever did.
Colonel Muadhen was also in charge of a brigade, which
had grown twice as large since he had been appointed to
command it.

In fact, the size of the Continental Army was stead-
ily increasing. This was only partly because all that
needle-sticking General Washington had ordered in
January actually seemed to have slowed down the advance of the smallpox. It was also due to the fact that
ordinary work was hard to find. The rich were constantly closing down their stores and great houses to
move to Canada, muttering about "revolutionary rabble" and "the madness of mobs" as they departed.

Seamus's brigade were informally called the Fighting Irish and they were one of several Gaelic-speaking
brigades—Irish immigrants from the West Counties,
where English was still little known, who had enlisted
in the Continental Army as soon as they discovered
that, when an insurrection has graduated to a rebellion
and gives promise of growing to a revolution, there is
not much secure employment being offered by the
Proprietor class.

The British and their Hessian mercenaries went on winning most battles. Colonel Muadhen did what he could to keep up morale by giving his troops stentorian orations in the tradition of Finn Mac Cumhail, made up of his own Gaelic translations of rhetorical high spots of the Declaration and the *Crisis* pamphlets by Tom Paine (b. 1737, teacher, sailor, customs agent &c). Since he had met Mr. Paine on a ship once, Colonel Muadhen improved the story and told the troops he had met Mr. Jefferson on the same ship, too, and both men were Irish and proud of it. He did not feel compelled to inform his troops that Tom Paine was at first intermittently, then frequently, and later continuously (albeit hilariously and cheerfully) intoxicated all across the Atlantic and confessed to having deserted his wife.

The troops believed Seamus's stories of these two great Irish rebels. Tom Jefferson sounded much like O'Lachlann, the rebel bard of Meath, and Tom Paine even more remarkably like Blind Raftery, the satirical bard of Kerry, by the time Seamus Muadhen was through translating them into the pungently idiomatic Gaelic of the Finn Mac Cumhail epics.

SUMMER SOLDIERS AND SUNSHINE PATRIOTS

When winter came and the Continental Army retreated to Valley Forge, like a whipped hound crawling to its kennel, Colonel Muadhen found it harder to keep up morale and inspire his troops with patriotic fervor. By the time of the Norse Yule or the anniversary of the birth of the late Redeemer of biblical renown, nearly three thousand men shuffled off this mortal coil (as a famous Saxon bard would have it) and it was perplexing for even an Irish orator to find a cheery word to say about that. Every morning, there were a hundred more corpses to be buried, victims of pneumonia, influenza, or some other side effect of the vicious weather. And every morning there were more deserters, men who vanished in the night, creeping past the sentries with the spectral silence and animal cunning of those who have absolutely determined and resolved to absent themselves from a less desirable environment to seek a more desirable one.

Dirty, sneaking cowards, Seamus thought. *I wonder when I'll have the sense to make a run for it and join them.*

NOBLEWOMAN FRETS, EDITOR BOOZES AND THEOSEXUAL SCANDAL BEGINS

Lady Maria Babcock's letter to the *London Gazette* questioning the validity of all-male juries in cases involving crimes against women had been judiciously phrased; it carefully avoided excesses of polemic or sarcasm, was closely reasoned, and made its points in a thoughtful and noninflammatory manner. The subject matter alone, however, would have disqualified it for publication on simple grounds of *good taste* and *common sense,* except that the editor, Weskit Fitzloosely, was taken suddenly drunk the day the letter arrived and, in a spirit of good clean fun, decided to print this crazy female rant just "to hear the animals howl," as he told his associates, weaving and staggering around the office and chortling hilariously at his merry prank.

Naturally, since there are many sober Christian souls in England, the immediate response was not as humorous as Weskit's mood when printing the first Feminist document in British history. Almost all readers, in fact, were incensed, and the majority were hopping mad. Some viewed with alarm. Some were grieved and wounded to read such French-sounding radicalism in a previously sound and sensible paper. Some enquired if Voltaire had taken over as editor, or was it the even more atheistic Diderot? Some took sharp exception to the lady's un-Christian notions. Some canceled subscriptions. Some raved. Some ranted. Some roared. Some fulminated. Some had cat fits, pseudolyncanthropy, and blind staggers. In one London suburb, some devout and pious Methodists burned "the Italian hoor" in effigy.

AMID FUROR, *LE VICE ANGLAIS* IS NOT NEGLECTED

Weskit Fitzloosely was hugely delighted. He had indeed made the animals howl, and, despite the canceled subscriptions, he had gained thousands of new readers, all of them delightfully daft and eager to express themselves in the letters column. Nothing had been so successful since Weskit himself had faked a letter from a nonexistent reader who confessed that he like being caned on the fundament by his wife and asked if others shared this taste, whereby similar confessions came in by the thousands and tens of thousands, lending some credence to the French view that this odd taste was indeed "the English vice." Mr. Fitzloosely decided to get drunk more often and see what new and daring editorial policies might strike him that way.

BUT WHAT WILL HER HUSBAND SAY?

Sir John Babcock, M.P., was equally enthusiastic. After his many years in Parliament, he was accustomed to controversy, unafraid of it, and was proud that Maria had the gift of arousing some glorious hell on her own.

Besides, Sir John was always glad to have a radical new idea. His father, Sir Edward Babcock, the jurist, had taught him to despise the religious biases that had kept so much of Europe at war for nearly three centuries; that was why John had become a Freemason and, eventually, a Deist; it was also why he dared to marry Maria even though she was then a Papist. He had learned on his own to hate colour bias, and had become the acknowledged leader of the antislavery faction of the Whig party. Now Maria had suddenly made him aware of a new bias he had never noticed before (perhaps because it was so omnipresent as to have become, as water is said to be for fishes, invisible): *gender bias.* A Whig with a new and controversial cause, in those days, was as happy as a thief with rubber pockets in a soup kitchen.

THEORIES OF ATLANTIS, SECRET CODES, AND ALLEGED FALL OF ROCK FROM SKY

John wrote a new bill, making juries open to women as well as to men. It received two votes in committee, one from a cohort in the antislavery movement who claimed Newton's laws of motion were coded into Shakespeare's plays in acrostic, and the other from a man who believed the Isle of Man was the lost Atlantis and Scotland was Homer's Hyperborea. The bill never got onto the floor of the House. That, of course, persuaded Sir John Babcock that he was right. In his experience, the smaller the minority to which he belonged, the more likely it was that he would be vindicated with the passing of time. On one issue, in fact, he was a minority of one—he had seen with his own eyes a large stone *fall out of the sky* five years ago, and the whole Royal Scientific Society was still laughing at him, because his only supporting witness was an Irishman and everybody knew the Irish were all drunken liars.

Because of Maria's letter and John's aborted bill, they became known in some circles as The Batty Babcocks, a sobriquet not without distinction in a nation where the aristocracy increasingly believed it their duty as well as their right to be eccentric.

The controversy roared along. Presbyterian ministers, for some reason, showed a special gift for recalling passages from the Papist, Thomas Aquinas (1225–74, auth. *Summa Theologica, Summa Contra Gentiles,* sanctified, beatified, glorified, *imprimatur, nihil obstat*), about the inferiority and irrationality of women, the curse of Eve, and the role of hierarchy (*viz.* authority and submission) in God's perfectly moral, perfectly rational creation. Church of England spokesmen were more apt to produce quotes from St. Paul about women keeping silence, or from Origen about the set of all women and the set of all sacks of dung and the isomorphism of aforesaid sets. The clergy as a whole, however, were equally gifted at documenting, beyond any peradventure of doubt, that the ideas of the Babcocks contradicted the most basic principles of Christianity as it had been preached and understood from the first century to the present.

THE VOICE OF THE PULPIT IS HEARD IN THE LAND

The issue was simple, all ordained clergy agreed: Christianity on one side, and on the other side the blasphemous Babcocks proclaiming heresies more libertine and ungodly than the rebels in the American colonies.

Maria was horrified at first, as she gradually realized that the clergy were not only sincere but were actually historically and doctrinally correct.

She had given birth to three children; she had nursed her brother, Carlo, when he was wounded by the scoundrel, Sigismundo Celine; she had been taught logic and science by a unique Mother Superior in a very liberal convent; she was adult and free of most illusions, especially since she had learned that John, for all his loving kindness and high ideals, was not above occasional infidelity.

Still, she was not prepared for the venom of the attacks on her sanity and morals provoked by her simple and reasonable letter, and she did not expect to be forced by logic and simple honesty to agree that, by either Catholic or Protestant standards, she was indeed both insane and illogical. The person who had called her "the worst heretic since Simon Magus himself" was quite simply correct. Her ideas were completely un-Christian in any objective historical reckoning of what Christianity meant.

ANALYSIS AND EXEGESIS ON HOLY WRIT BY OUR MARIA

Maria, in fact, mulled over these attacks a bit too much, perhaps; she brooded on them, she became obsessed, somewhat, with the fact that the most vicious denunciations all seemed to have been written by clergymen.

Clergy*men*.

That was the second step in Maria Babcock's development into becoming the most revolutionary thinker in a century of revolutionists. She began to think critically about the reverend gentlemen of the clergy. She *analyzed* the arguments contained in their fulminations against her, and their clear proofs that she had contradicted Holy Writ and all Christian tradition.

Mother Ursula, Maria's convent teacher, had made a strong impression—that was why Maria's first child was named Ursula. The abbess of the Saint Theophobia school for young ladies had tried to teach her pupils algebra, trigonometry, geometry, natural science, and other unladylike subjects, including *logic* and those counterfeits of true logic called *rhetoric*. Maria could see the difference between a real and unique horse with real individual characteristics and the Ideal Platonic Horse, and she understood the vast gap between real horseshit on a farmer's boots and Ideal Platonic Horseshit in academic philosophy. Since marrying a Deist, living in England among Protestants, and learning folk medicine from Old Kyte, Lousewartshire's local witch, Maria had become somewhat detached from mere dogma. The old abbess, Mother Ursula, had made Maria a more independent thinker than she had intended.

A LITERARY VENTURE IS ANNOUNCED

Maria became convinced that *gender bias* was not incidental to Christianity but was the very essence of the Christian faith. The reverend gentlemen of the clergy had absolutely and totally convinced her of that, in their polemics against her.

When she told John she was writing a book, he was proud of her. He had always wanted to write a damned fat book of some sort himself, if Parliament had not kept him so busy, and he thought it was wonderful to have at least one Author in the family.

When Maria read him the first ten pages he started laughing on page one, laughed louder on each succeeding page, and ended up, when she finished, looking as gravely serious as an Archbishop explaining what he and the mezzo-soprano were doing in the choir loft.

DISGUISE RECOMMENDED BY M.P.

"I say, love of my life," John said finally, "have you, um, ah, considered using a *nom de plume?*"

In fact, although Maria was angry and intense about her new attitudes toward the clergy, she was not a damned fool and had thought of several possible *noms de plume*.

AND SHE WAS THE MOTHER OF ISAAC, NO DOUBT

And so, early in 1778, all concern about the war in the American colonies was suddenly swept aside briefly by the appearance of a highly original theological treatise titled, with deceptive simplicity, *A Moistness in the Wind* and attributed to one Sarah Beckersniff.

CENSORSHIP FOLLOWED BY PIRACY! HOT STUFF!

The first printing sold out in two days. The second printing, rushed by a printer who could not believe his good luck, appeared a week later and was seized by the sheriff and burned by the public hangman. Parliament had stampeded into action even faster than the printer, as soon as they saw the first edition. The printer, to escape arrest, changed his name and relocated his presses in Paris, but several others, wise enough not to advertise, printed pirate copies and sent hawkers to peddle them in alleys. It was estimated that by 1780 over sixty such pirate editions had appeared, of which only seven copies are now known to exist— one in the Vatican Library, one in the Bibliothèque Nationale in Paris, one in the Library of Congress, one at Harvard University, one in the Kinsey Research Institute, one in the private collection of Gershon Legman, and one, of course, at Miskatonic University in Arkham.

ON THE ENDOWMENTS OF DIVINITY— HOW MUCH?

A Moistness in the Wind addressed the issue of whether or not God had a penis and, if not, what was the source of the attitude of reverence that the Christian clergy exhibited toward that organ, rather than the liver or pancreas or aorta. It said, among other things, that everybody more civilized than "the Methodists, the Howlers & the Ranters'' now agreed that God was a spirit and it seemed "impossible for Reason or Imagination to call up a *clear & vivid* Image of what it might mean for a Spirit to have a *virile Member,* or what such a *ghostly Organ* itself would look like to perception'' and it enquired, not delicately, into what must be supposed in logic to be the dimensions in inches or feet or *miles* of the phallus of a cosmic be-ing. It argued learnedly and sometimes pedantically that if God did not possess such ''a gross *physickal* Organ,'' it was illogical, ungrammatical, and "con-trary to Anatomy and proper Usage" to refer to God as "He" or to speak of God in male metaphors as "Lord" or "King."

QUALIFICATIONS OF THE CLERGY CHALLENGED

The gnomically titled *Moistness in the Wind* went even further in examining the sexual, the biological, and, very specifically, the concretely anatomical pre-suppositions of Christian dogma. For instance,

There is not one church in Christendom, from sun-drenched Egypt in the south to rain-drown'd Ireland, or from the icy steppes of Russia to the transatlantic Amer-ican colonies, but that *believes* and *fervently espouses* the Doctrine that only a Male may be a Priest, a Preacher or a minister of the Gospel. On all else—on every Doctrine the devious human Mind can devise or invent to compli-cate and obscure the simple *Message* of Jesus—they are in disagreement, one with another, in a manner *fearfully* ferocious, cold-heartedly murderous, wickedly *unholy* & totally implacable, but on the Question of what Manner of Human may be appoint'd or accept'd to the Clergy, there is a *Singular* and *Curious* Uniformity on the perverse and peculiar doctrine that such a human being must be in possession of that organ—blasphemously and absurdly attributed to God by the pronoun "He"—which Doctors in learn'd tones call the glans penis and which in everyday language is called, in more homely fashion, the *Willy.*

Now, this Doctrine is so remarkable and yet so Universal that nobody hitherto hath question'd it, it is generally consider'd a "mystery of the faith" and beyond human *Reason.* A person born with a Willy may represent a God who also hath a Willy and, upon earth, speak for that God, and a person, of equal intelligence and talents, without the *qualification* of a *Willy* is forever debarr'd from such Holy Office.

NO WOMEN OR SISSIES NEED APPLY FOR HOLY ORDERS

But, my Lords and gentle Ladies of the kingdom, in the name of humanity, in the name of reason, what is so special, so miraculous, so *sacred* about a Willy that it confers this strange potential *Holiness* upon its possessor? Does God have no other trait signifying Holiness except "His" Willy? Why is it that the meanest, dullest, most vicious and ignorant Man in the land may always consider the Possibility that if he reforms slightly, or even pretends to reform, he may someday be a *Priest* of Christ, while the most learn'd, the most pious, the most devout Woman who exists must always remember, and can never forget for a moment, that she is *disqualified* from Religious Office for this one reason and this reason only, that she does not possess the *Wonderful* and *all-important* Willy so central to Christian ideas of Holiness?

What is there in the Willy that makes one a *Representative* of the Divine, and what is there in lack of a Willy that makes one forever profane? Are we to believe the Willy itself is some special Sign or *Symbol* of divinity, of the infinite Godhead Itself? That God's wisdom and *loving* Kindness and Infinite Power are secondary and unimportant, and would render even God less Godly if not accompanied by the Holy & Paramountly *Omnipotent* Willy? The priest, it hath been claimed, represents Christ, and, again, one must pointedly enquire: Is our *great love & adoration* for Jesus based on his infinite Mercy, his wisdom, his *noble* Sacrifice on the *Cross,* his forgiveness of his enemies, his countless qualities & *virtues* that make him an Emblem of Goodness, or is the most important *fact* about him simply this, that he was in possession of that which every Vagabond & Thief also hath, the Willy? Is this not the significance of the curious text to be found in Deuteronomy, chapter 23, verse 1—*viz.,* in plain language, even one born Male may not enter the temple if the *divine* Willy be destroy'd by Accident or deliberate Malice?

ITHYPHALLIC EIDOLONS

A Moistness in the Wind went on to discuss, in explicit detail, the ithyphallic statues of Osiris and Pan and Hermes to be found around the Mediterranean, pointing out that these divinities were depicted with Willies "three times, or on occasion, even four times *Longer* and *Thicker* and generally more Gargantuan than the norm for the mortal Male" and asked if "the ancients believed, what these *Holy* Statues (for so they were in their own Time) strongly suggest—*viz.,* that the *greater* the *Mass* of the Willy, the greater the *Divinity* indwelling." Did this idea survive in the Christian conviction that it required a Willy to represent the authority of God on earth? The next paragraph created considerable hilarity in Protestant England, but even so its implications were unbearable and unthinkable to Christians of all persuasions—

WOULD HIS HOLINESS BE HOLY WITHOUT THE MYSTIC WILLY?

We must ask, in all solemnity, is the Pope himself, the most prestigious, pugnacious, awe-inspiring, *wealthy,* and *Gorgeously* Dress'd of all Christian clergymen (and the very Vicar of Christ on Earth, to his devout followers) elevated to that rank because he possesses the Divine attribute of the *Willy?* For, surely, he could never have become even a *parish priest* in Palermo without a Willy, and so could never have advanced to the rank of Bishop, Archbishop &c and eventually to his present *Eminence* without a Willy. This, then, is why we have never seen in history (or anywhere but in the Tarot cards) a Female Pope—the magick & marvelous Willy appears, to the Christians as to the Pagans, the emblem of the *Kingdom* and the *Power* and the *Glory* of God. Without it, the Pope could not reign, nor would any Catholic listen to his religious opinions. But if this be the essense and *Epitomy* of the Christian Faith, why not follow it to its ineluctable *Logical* Conclusion? Why should not he with the Largest Willy of all hold the highest rank, since it be in the Willy that *Godliness* resideth? Should not "pilgrims with short muskets" be restrict'd to the lower ranks of Holy Orders, those only gifted with Tools of more Formidable size be elevated to Bishopricks &c, and He alone with the most *terrific & Gargantuan* Willy in the population be elevated to such status as that of Archbishop of Canterbury or *Supreme* Pontiff?

BAD TASTE REACHES NEW HEIGHTS; VICE OF ONAN ALLEGED

Even in that pre-Freudian era, *A Moistness in the Wind* did not hesitate to explore what Maria (a.k.a. Sarah Beckersniff) called "the strange, *obscure* & sub-

terranean psychology of the *Worship* of the Willy.''
This perhaps did more harm to English imperialism
than the entire career of General George Washington.
Some connection between compulsive adolescent masturbation and life-long commitment to the mystique of
male domination—some ithyphallic mania—was more
than mildly hinted at in passages like:

> I am told on good Authority and verily believe that boys
> approaching the *Cusp* of Manhood, at about ages twelve
> to fourteen, often develop a superstitious Awe and sense
> of *Magick* about this Willy of theirs; some, it is said, even
> give the organ a Name of *Endearment,* and regard the Willy
> with a truly *infatuated* Love, and those especially addicted
> to self-enjoyment grow so *Fervent* in this singular and sol-
> itary Passion that learned Doctors have feared for their
> sanity. But what are we to think of *adult* males who have
> never outgrown this superstitious *Narcissism* and still ver-
> ily believe the ''magickal'' Willy to be the very Emblem
> and Significator of the *Divine* upon Earth? Have they re-
> mained entranc'd and enthrall'd—virtually *Mesmeriz'd*—by
> the object of their first ardent erotic feelings? Where else
> cometh the strange & unanimous conviction of the rev.
> clergy that this organ alone is proof of Godliness & *Vir-
> tue?* Yea, I suspect and dare to proclaim, indeed, that this
> Willy-worship explaineth why the very word ''Virtue'' it-
> self cometh from the root, *vir.,* designating possession of
> the Male *member* or all-powerful Willy.

IT IS WITH SORROW WE REPORT THE DEATH OF A GREAT EMPIRE

The effects of Maria's booklet were slow at first,
like an avalanche, but, like an avalanche, multiplied
in momentum with time. By 1779, the Phi Beta Kappa
Society of Yale was debating *in public* whether women

had intellectual capacities equal to men (Phi Beta Kappa of Harvard that year was debating whether Adam had a navel, thereby beginning the long tradition of always being intellectually a few centuries behind Yale). By 1792, *A Moistness in the Wind* was followed by Mary Wollstonecraft's somewhat less radical *Vindication of the Rights of Women,* which had the demerit of being discussable in polite society and therefore had less real effect than the banned, shunned, forbidden, and loathed Beckersniff blasphemies, which everybody really read.

By 1800, there had been over a thousand clandestine printings of this grossly indecent Beckersniff booklet. Because of the scandal it had provoked, the infamy of *A Moistness in the Wind* survived all the censors and book burners; it was never discussed in decent circles, and never had the overt notoriety of Wollstonecraft's *Vindication,* but even in the Victorian Age, Professor Pokorny found (see his invaluable *The Necronomicon and Other Unspeakable Texts*) at least thirty thousand printings appeared, especially in the vicinity of Oxford, where it was a great favorite with giggling undergraduates.

A mortal blow had been struck to the very stronghold of British manhood. Even those who laughed and believed they were reading a variety of philosophical pornography were undermined. The Willy itself, accepted as natural by the pagans and clothed in glamorous Diabolism by the Christian Fathers, had abruptly become merely comical, and authority based on nothing else but possession of a Willy seemed not only obscene but childish. Self-confidence ebbed; virility withered; despite Kipling and Haggard, a melancholy, long, withdrawing roar was noticed as Anglo-Saxon manhood tottered, staggered, and stumbled.

INDIFFERENT DEITY (WITH OR WITHOUT WILLY) PROVOKES CELTIC DOUBT

Colonel Muadhen had had a bad eye going into the War for Independence—from an altercation with the British Army in Dun Laoghaire—and now he had a bad leg from the wound at Brandywine. In Valley Forge, he woke up cold every morning and went to sleep chilled every night. Washington's vocabulary became more greenly empurpled and polychromatic than ever. If they ever survived this winter, Seamus thought wearily, they would just meet the Brits again and get beaten again.

When General von Steuben was through drilling the troops that day, Seamus called his Fighting Irish together and gave them another inspirational Gaelic sermon on liberty and sacrifice and heroism. He became rhetorical, as only one speaking classic Gaelic can be rhetorical, and gave a resonant translation of Mr. Jefferson's argument that Nature and Nature's God were on the side of the rebellion.

He almost believed it himself, when he was finished.

But among all the dying men in Valley Forge, Seamus Muadhen, who had always wanted to avoid politics and had been warned by a Sinister Italian that History was even worse than ordinary politics, privately wondered if Nature and Nature's God were any less mythical than the Pope and the Pope's God.

Christ on the cross cried out, "My God, my God, why hast thou forsaken me?" *And we are all such damned eejits,* Seamus thought, *that we never remember that no giant Hand reached down to help him and he hung there until he died?*

"My God, my God, why hast thou forsaken me?"
he asked the heavens, experimentally. The sky remained blue and empty and indifferent, and the cold
still made him shiver with pain.

Nature and Nature's God, Seamus thought hope-
lessly, *don't give a fart in their knickers about human
beings.*

TWO YANKS IN PARIS: JOHN GROWS GRUMPY, BEN MAKES WHOOPEE

In Paris, Ben Franklin and John Adams are negotiating with the nervous young man whom Major General de Lafayette always called "the fat boy"—King
Louis XVI. Or, at least, they are trying to negotiate
with him, or his ministers, or somebody. The fat boy
was still trying to avoid making up his mind what to
do about M. Franklin and M. Adams and the Americans in general.

To damage England, since it appears impossible to
destroy the damned place, is always a paramount goal
of French politics, and the fat boy has allowed M.
Sartines and other advisers to persuade him to send
quite a few francs, through clandestine routes created
by M. Beaumarchais's irregular little bank, to America. But Franklin and Adams want a lot more, and the
fat boy does not want to spend recklessly on any one
project, and he also does not want to let the English
know what he is doing, and so he keeps Franklin and
Adams dangling in uncertainty.

Adams fretted, fumed, fulminated, and finally decided the French were a detestable people. He set off
on his own, without congressional approval, to Holland, where he planned to borrow millions of guilders
from the tough old Amsterdam bankers. He was an

honest man, and his cause was just, and he did not think it possible that he could be refused. That was how he had won the acquittal of an English officer in a Massachusetts court, and how he had persuaded the Continental Congress to vote for Independence. He was an honest man and his cause was just, so he knew he would not fail.

Franklin decided that delay was the normal course of politics and that John Adams was some kind of apocalyptical visionary who should be writing tracts on Calvinist eschatology at Harvard Divinity School; he settled down to enjoy Paris and wait for the king to make up his mind. Meanwhile, he acquired a dozen or so delicious new mistresses—perhaps only average for a celebrity in Paris, but not unimpressive for a man in his seventies—and even had the honor of initiating the great Voltaire into Freemasonry, under the auspices of the fashionable Grand Orient Lodge.

LE BARRE CASE RECALLED; DID HE LOSE HIS HEAD UNJUSTLY?

François-Marie Arouet de Voltaire (b. 1694, essayist, novelist, poet, heresiarch) returned to Paris almost as a walking historical monument; most of the ideas for which he was exiled are now not only *chic* but *bon ton*. The fat boy, it appears, was induced to grant amnesty to the aging *philosophe* (Arouet de Voltaire is now eighty-two) by the ever-persuasive M. Sartines, the clever little fishmonger's son who is now chief of the secret police and untitled Minister of Everything in General. It is a shrewd move. The Church thunders and roars, but the people at large have fallen in love with the old man who, exiled in Switzerland for a dog's age, has kept up a continuous polemic against all the abuses of the feudal system.

For over a decade, M. Voltaire has concentrated his fire on the Inquisition, an increasingly unpopular institution already abolished in a few Italian states. He harps on the case of the chevalier le Barre, who was beheaded in '66 on extremely dubious evidence; he has raised the young man's ghost, and le Barre, in death, stalks France like an exterminating angel.

Even some of the Dominicans themselves are beginning to wish the Holy Office would be a little more careful in pronouncing verdicts. You would think it was England or some other Protestant pest-hole, the way people talk about due process these days. Voltaire has changed the trajectory of Catholic history.

When the octogenarian atheist or deist (nobody in France is very clear about the difference) arrives in Paris, the scene is like a Cecil de Mille spectacle two centuries in advance. The mob goes mad, especially those who don't have the foggiest notions of the old relic's philosophy; he has challenged kings, bishops, bankers, all of *them*, and he has survived—that is enough to make him a national hero.

THE GRAND ORIENT LODGE

The duc d'Orleans—"the friend of the people," as he is called—sets about recruiting the champion of Free Thought into Freemasonry at once. Voltaire agrees, placidly, and the great, gray, searching eyes of M. Sartines pop open a bit wider. He adds another note to his file on Orleans and the Grand Orient Lodge of Egyptian Freemasonry.

M. Franklin is requested to act as Worshipful Master of the East in the initiation, and is happy to oblige.

It is a great moment when the hoodwink is removed, and the most famous Rationalist of the age sees that he had been engaged in revolutionary rituals with the most famous Scientist of the Age—the man who hurled lightning bolts at the Vatican faces the man who tamed the lightning with a key on a kite string.

MATHEMATICIAN TRACES FUTURE TRAJECTORIES

After the initiation, some say, M. Voltaire and M. Franklin had a banquet with the Marquis de Condorcet, France's most gifted mathematician, and discussed science and philosophy.

M. Condorcet, in the course of this symposium, asserted that with the steady advance of medicine (moving faster everywhere, as the steady decline of the Inquisition acclerated) a time would come when every disease would be abolished. M. Franklin agreed, but M. Voltaire said it would take longer than they realized.

M. Condorcet then went further and said that, in a thousand years, when all governments were staffed by Freemasons and the last doddering old priest had been killed by a brick falling from the last decaying and deserted church, medicine would advance to the point where death itself would be abolished. M. Franklin agreed again—he had written a bit on that subject himself, diplomatically leaving out the necessity of abolishing Christianity before this could be accomplished. M. Voltaire was again skeptical. Life extension was possible, he agreed, but immortality was a Christian superstition, and unworthy of scientific minds.

M. Condorcet then grew more enthusiastic—they

were on their third bottle of wine by then and, as a mathematician, he had a better head for third-order differentials than for fermented distillates. He announced that he could foresee major reforms in the next *century* alone. M. Franklin listened, spellbound, as M. Condorcet pictured for them a world in which education was free for all, boys and girls alike, and schools were taught by rational, well-educated men and women, not by narrow-minded priests and nuns. A world in which insurance companies, some perhaps run by private investors and some perhaps by the state, would pay decent compensation to those injured and disabled, and even to those unemployed by economic recession. A world in which the state would loan money for scientific and technological research not even imaginable today, perhaps even to fly to the moon. A world in which every city had free libraries, like the one M. Franklin had started in Philadelphia, and the state and private investors would offer "illness insurance," so nobody would die for lack of money to pay the doctors. M. Franklin agreed that all of this might happen in a century, but some of it would probably take two centuries.

SKEPTICAL DISSENT: SOUTH ITALY SINGLED OUT AS PALEOLITHIC

M. Voltaire said it couldn't happen until those rational teachers Condorcet imagined had replaced religious orders in the educational system, and that would take a thousand years in the civilized nations, five thousand years in the Middle East, a hundred thousand years in the Orient, two hundred thousand in northern Italy, and a million years in Rome and Naples.

PROLETARIAN PERSPECTIVE

While the philosophers sup and speculate, half a mile away a joiner or woodworker named Jean Jacques Jeder plays with his newborn son. Jeder, who had turned to crime during a period of unemployment in 1771, had become honest again later the same year when employment became available once more, and had turned looter and incendiary during the passions of the "Grain War" in '75, and has been an honest man again in the two years of comparative prosperity since then.

But Jeder remembers the Grain War. He remembers the exhilaration of the days when the mob, not the army, controlled Paris. He remembers the horrors at the end of it all, when the State reasserted its Authority and expressed its Revenge by hanging selected scapegoats. He had started reading the revolutionary pamphleteers after the hangings—his friend, Luigi Duccio, the stonecutter from Naples, always had the illegal pamphlets for sale—and nowadays he is reading all the news from America with special zeal. He is studying the events over there with attention to detail, as he has learned to study blueprints when working on a house.

America is a very interesting blueprint to Jean Jacques Jeder, and Luigi Duccio, and other radical workers in Paris.

TURN BACK, TURN BACK!

At the University of Paris, the distinguished visiting professor of metaphysics from Germany, Dr. Fritz Cyprus, had just completed his monumental and influential treatise, *The Path Backward*. Even more radical and extremist than Rousseau, Dr. Cyprus argues that progress is an illusion, medicine is the enemy of health, reason is irrational, and the Dark Ages were the epitome of enlightenment. Since he is German, this is embedded in prose so formidable that everybody is staggered by it, except the irascible Voltaire.

A few weeks before his death, the old skeptic wrote a review, showing his customary antipathy to macaronic metaphysics. Cyprus, he says, "glorifies everything about the dark ages except their filth, ignorance, disease, barbarism and superstition, which is to say he admires everything about those days except what was really happening then." But Voltaire will soon be unfashionable, and Dr. Cyprus will be a major influence on Romanticism, fascism, and all forms of antirationalism in the next two centuries.

THE INEVITABLE MOTHER-IN-LAW JOKE

In the Bastille, poor old Father Henri Benoit finally found a new philosophical companion to replace the vanished Sigismundo Celine. Even more of a heretic than Celine, and much more tenacious in argument, this new one, but therefore a worthy antagonist. Debate was more stimulating to the old priest than agreement, after twenty-three years in confinement.

Father Benoit's new friend was Donatien-Aldonse François de Sade, a short blonde marquis from the south, who had been imprisoned for blasphemy, profanity, sedition, heresy, atheism, buggery, sodomy, poor usage of controlled substances, and annoying his mother-in-law.

De Sade cheerfully told the priest he was guilty on all counts, and unrepentant. "You should meet my mother-in-law," he said, explaining the only offense that had gotten him in serious trouble, his other peccadilloes being normal for his class.

PRIEST INVOKES DIVINE PLAN, EMPIRICIST PLUGS FOR MECHANISM

The priest and the marquis spent many pleasant afternoons in the courtyard discussing whether the universe were a mindless machine or the creation of a loving God. The priest argued in terms of philosophy and metaphysics, but the marquis was temperamentally an empiricist and argued always in terms of what the world was actually like. "Look at the smallpox," he would say. "Kills a few hundred thousand every month all over Europe. What kind of Benevolent Intelligence decided to give us that as a birthday present? Did your merciful and omnipotent God have constipation that day, and put him in a foul enough mood to perpetuate such a fiendish joke at our expense?"

"But the physicians now seem to have a cure for the smallpox," Benoit would say. "Surely much inspirations are given to human minds by a Higher Intelligence."

"I have talked to more physicians than you," de Sade would reply. "The bright young ones who are making all the radical discoveries are atheists like me. They say the body is a machine. No soul inside, just gears and levers of complicated sorts. They cure more patients with that atheistic idea than all the prayers of the dark ages combined have ever been reputed to cure."

"The compassion that inspires those doctors is all the proof I need that man receives divine guidance from above," the priest would say, returning the ball to the marquis.

"Their compassion did no good until they started thinking materialistically," de Sade would bounce back.

And so on. It kept both the old priest and the young nobleman amused during the years of incarceration. Each knew he would never convince the other.

NOTABLE VICTORY RECORDED

By the Spring of 1778, the Continental Army was beginning to rise from its symbolic death at Valley Forge and at last started to give the British some real problems. Colonel Seamus Muadhen didn't have to turn Jefferson and Paine into Raftery and O'Lachlann to stir up the enthusiasm of his Celtic brigade; there was optimism in the air, perhaps because the Continental Army had survived longer than any rational mind could have expected.

In June came the battle of Monmouth and their greatest victory in the war thus far. Military authorities later explained why the Continentals should not have won that battle: In military logic, it was an impossible victory. General Charles Lee, in the middle of the battle, had exactly the same view as these later experts and ordered a retreat (for which General Washington later court-martialed him, after assuring him in personal conversation that he was by God, sir, the most yellow-bellied cur ever begotten by a cowardly boar hog upon a mentally retarded polecat and had no more right to his uniform than a buggering idiot offspring of a whore and a trained pony) but the Brits had turned tail and run, and the Continentals were on the attack, and that made all the difference.

Colonel Muadhen congratulated his troops afterwards, in Gaelic. He told them that not all the battles in Europe where Irish "wild geese" had distinguished themselves for bravery were as glorious as this victory, and that when General John ("Gentleman Johnny") Burgoyne finally stopped running he would tell everybody in England it was those wild Irish from Connaught who had smashed his troops that day.

He wanted to say a lot more things like that but his voice was drowned out by the screams from the medical tents, where men with serious leg wounds were having their legs sawed off to save them from dying of gangrene.

FAT BOY DECIDES TO MOVE, DUTCH UNCLES SHOW SOFT SPOT

King Louis XVI decided finally to recognize American independence, which Franklin took as proof that his policy of patient diplomacy was finally beginning to work.

Meanwhile, the obnoxious Adams returned from Holland with a loan of 1.3 million dollars for the American colonists. Nobody else was ever able to understand how he talked those Dutch bankers into such a wildly speculative venture, but he himself knew it was because he was honest and his cause was just.

LITERARY EFFORT BY NOBLEMAN POSITS FOUR ARCHETYPES

In the Bastille, the Marquis de Sade is writing a book that is partly a novel and partly a philosophical treatise and partly the result of his meditations on why Father Benoit, an intelligent man, still believed in God and Justice after being locked in his hell-hole for twenty-four years. In this book, de Sade hopes to show

how the world actually operates, what sort of men govern it, and what motivates them.

He has made his major characters a Count, to represent the old landed nobility; a Banker, to represent the rising bourgeois class; a Bishop, to represent the Church Militant; and a Judge, to represent the State itself as the supreme authority, which may punish and murder whomever it chooses. In short, four men symbolizing the four powers that control France at present—and, incidentally, have imprisoned him for his own sexual and intellectual eccentricities.

Sade's *magnum opus* is called *The 120 Days of Sodom,* and its thesis is that the world is a cattle farm owned and operated by madmen. His Count and Bishop and Banker and Judge are demonic cowherds who spend their 120 days of vacation contemplating various intricate and exquisite forms of torture that they may inflict on the herds they own—the poor, the helpless, the weak, and, especially, the female.

He reads portions of this to old Father Benoit occasionally, vastly enjoying the priest's horrified reaction.

"My spirit is entirely scientific," Sade tells the old man. "I observe carefully and report accurately. I invent nothing, since I am deficient in imagination and gifted only at close observation and analysis. These four men of mine are the types who rule the world. If I am correct in my materialistic view, Nature has selected them. If I am incorrect, and above Nature is your God, then that God has, for his own obscure reasons, left the world in their custody."

The priest protests—although he has been unjustly imprisoned for as many years as many people's whole lives, he still will not accept that there is not justice or reason in the world. He argues that Sade is embittered and cynical, and probably just a frustrated idealist tormenting himself.

"I am the second cousin of the king," Sade says simply. "I have had opportunities most philosophers have never enjoyed, to peek and pry into the centers of power and make a scientific study of the men who dwell there, for whom power is an aphrodisiac. I exaggerate nothing. Every battle in every war has all the atrocities I describe, and there is no year without a battle somewhere because the men who run the world are men exactly like my four archetypes."

FROM DIVERSION TO SUBVERSION

The materialistic marquis "warms to his subject" as the writing proceeds: *The 120 Days of Sodom* swells from an anatomy to an encyclopedia. He has become the Diderot of the unconscious; he catalogs every twist and turn. Machiavelli told only the politics of the ruling elites—Sade has unmasked their inner drives. He is convinced he is writing a veritable masterpiece, the first truthful textbook on power and pain ever composed. At times, he even thinks of wild plans to smuggle the manuscript out of the Bastille and have it published, to show the world its own leering face in his polished looking glass.

The marquis' empirical mentality has turned the project from mere satire to social (or antisocial) science of a sort. As he catalogs fifty diverse techniques to violently abort a pregnant woman while causing her maximum prolonged agony in the process, he is also arguing that, in a Godless and mechanical universe, such projects make as much sense as anything else because they have as much meaning as anything else: namely, no sense and no meaning at all.

He knows—he never pretends not to know—that these monstrous creatures, the Count and Banker and Judge and Bishop, are all extensions of his own inner being. But he still claims, and believes, that they are also mirrors of what he has seen in the seats of power of the world.

A philosopher by necessity—prison does that for you—the marquis was no longer interested in perversion as diversion.

He has discovered perversion as subversion.

OPTIMIST SEES DONUT, PESSIMIST SEES HOLE, MYSTIC SEES MOEBIUS STRIP

The Marquis de Condorcet never stopped thinking and writing about a world that could be designed rationally to make for the maximum happiness of the maximum number of people, and many of his projects indeed came to pass in the next two hundred years. The Marquis de Sade never stopped thinking and writing about a world that could be designed rationally to make for the maximum horror and pain for the maximum number of people, and many of his projects also came to pass in the next two-hundred years.

Sigismundo Celine, in the woods of Ohio, meditated. To him all phenomena were real in some sense, unreal in some sense, meaningless in some sense, real and meaningless in some sense, unreal and meaningless in some sense, and real and unreal and meaningless in some sense.

DECLINE OF WILLY-WORSHIP AND RISE OF THATCHERISM

As the Victorian Age was replaced by the Age of Anxiety, the Beckersniff blasphemy continued to be an underground best-seller in Oxford and Cambridge, and whether God's Willy was either ghostly and Gargantuan or (conversely) ghoulishly nonexistent remained a favorite topic of speculation.

By 1950, the British Empire was obviously on the edge of mortal collapse. By 1968, there appeared in America and quickly spread back to Europe a variety of Radical Feminism that held that *possession*, not absense, of a Willy, irrespective of all other intellectual or moral traits, rendered a person vicious, vile, and subhuman.

By 1986—210 years after Maria Babcock became a revolutionary—there was virtually nothing left of the British Empire but six countries in the north of Ireland.

Presiding over the ruin was a prime minister who had risen to power entirely without the mystical Willy.

Book Two

△

Anything that doesn't kill me makes me stronger.
—Nietzsche
The Twilight of the Idols

△

7. The Wilderness Diary of Sigismundo Celine

Ohio 1776–78

A universe without a monarch or a parliament

Intellectual passions are more bewitching than love affairs, which is why they last longer. A man can adore a woman until she changes or grows surly, but he can be madly infatuated with a Theory all his life.

When the Pope sits on the chamber pot to shit, does he believe in his own infallibility? Does not every imposter occasionally recognize his own hairy, homely humanity? Perhaps not; worn long enough, sometimes the Mask of Authority becomes the man. Even looking in a mirror, he will see the sacred Mask and not his own ordinary human face.

N.B. It is not only the mighty who wear Masks. To be born in Napoli is to form a Neapolitan Mask before age six, I estimate. Similarly, those who grew up in Paris and London never cease to wear the Masks of the Parisian and the Londoner.

The study of psychology should be a history of the

metamorphoses of men and women into their habitual
Masks.

The Catholic wears a Catholic Mask at all times;
just look at the Neapolitan whores with crucifixes
around their necks. The Protestant also cannot remove
the Protestant Mask. Etc. Most comic of all; the Rationalist tries to wear the Mask of Reason even when
everybody else can see he is in the grip of a furious
passion.

There is no complete theory of *anything*. The damnable habit of giving children examinations in which
every question has a "true" or "false" answer has
conditioned us to think everything in the universe is
"true" or "false." In experience, most things emerge
out of Chaos, confuse and muddle us for a while, and
vanish into uncertainty again before we know what
they were or if they're coming back. The world is a
phalanx of maybes in which a handful of trues and
falses can occasionally be found.

We create our Masks, as God allegedly made the
world, out of nothing. In both cases, the nothingness
sometimes shows through.

It is quite easy to make friends with the wolves,
contrary to popular lore. Respect their territory, and
they will respect yours. It is impossible to negotiate
similarly with the fleas: that appears to be a fight to
the death.

Today, suddenly, I encountered a quite large brown-
ish bear in the woods. I was careful not to do anything
threatening (I had my rifle, but did not want to be

forced to shoot so noble a beast). Some ancient instinct told me not to run away. I pretended to ignore the huge animal, as if I had more important affairs on my mind. Then I saw out of the corner of my eye that the bear was doing exactly the same pantomime: he was using identical body signals—the same body "language," I might even say—to signify that I was not of any concern to a bear of his royal stature. We moved off, in opposite directions, all the time signaling that we were too busy to be bothered with lesser creatures. I would call this a case of Mask as body language.

Only later did I realize that I have seen dogs use that body language when they do not wish to fight. The implications of this simple experience are so staggering that I can scarcely formulate my own thoughts clearly. What it seems to suggest is that if dogs, bears, humans, and some other creatures have a common preverbal "language," then we also have a common *ancestor*.

The thought of the unity of life will not leave me. The wolves have a "king," just like the Neapolitans or French, etc., and His Lupine Majesty wears the Mask of authority in all that he does. I communicate well enough with the wolves that they come around more and more often to beg food. I communicated very eloquently with that bear, and he with me. All those statues I saw in North Africa of men or gods with animal heads suggest that some people have had this insight long before me—the human in the animal, the animal in the human. Buffon toys with this thought in his *Natural History,* and speaks of the possible evolution of life from a common source, but then he dismisses the idea as improbable. Did his great analytic mind really reject such a stupendous concept so myopically or did he just remember two unscientific facts: (a) the Inquisitors would read his words later and (b) he was not fireproof?

There is no governor anywhere and we are all relatives. Whenever I smoke the medicine herbs with Miskasquamic I can communicate with trees and that is not "hallucination." Animal and vegetable are cousins! Take off the Mask of humanity, as St. Francis did, and even rodents and roses talk to you, and you to them, in a language older than words.

Am I on the edge of a great discovery or am I going cracked from living alone too long? At times like this it is best to forget philosphy for a while and turn my mind back to music. Logic claims to *know*—it is the bastard son of priestcraft—but art, thank God, only aspires to share an experience.

Melody, harmony, counterpoint: I do not regret the years I spent learning these disciplines, but they are fundamentally irrelevant. If music ceases to be wonderful nonsense, it will not console the tormented heart.

The function of law and theology are the same: to keep the poor from taking back by violence what the rich have stolen by cunning.

The longer one is alone, the easier it is to hear the song of the earth. Yes, yes, yes: I am not going cracked, I am merely leaving human Masks behind. The wilderness is where truth is naked and hypocrisy has not been invented.

* * *

Nothing of any importance can be taught. It can only be learned, and with blood and sweat.

The function of Law? The recitation of the unintelligible by the unscrupulous to empty the purses of the unwary. The function of theology? The recitation of the incomprehensible by the unspeakable to pick the pockets of the unthinking.

If lawyers had been present on Mount Sinai, the Ten Commandments would have twelve hundred amendments, all summing to the conclusion: The rich may ignore these rules, the poor will be hanged if they violate the smallest subordinate clause.

The wisest line Shakespeare ever penned is in *Henry VI, Part II,* Act IV, Scene 2, line 85: "The first thing we do, let's kill all the lawyers."

The greatest thing about masturbation is that it is always available. I wager that many a condemned man has consoled himself this way during the night before his execution.

If carpenters had the ethics of lawyers, our chairs would all fall apart. If plumbers had the ethics of priests, everything would leak—but that would be called "miraculous moisture." I never fully appreciated plain men who talk straight and do honest work until I built my own cabin.

There is no law in nature, and therefore no bribery or corruption. There are no priests here, and therefore no sinners. A thousand miles from Man and History I can see that Nature is cyclical, meaningless, and without morality or malice.

Original Sin did not enter the world through disobedience but through imagination. It was the work of the ancient priest who wrote Genesis. Before that, men and women were as innocent and shameless as my friends the wolves.

A politician is a Mask with greed behind it. A priest is a Mask with Will to Power behind it.

Masturbation is not the happiest form of sexuality, but the most advisable for him who wants to be alone and think. I detect the aroma of this pleasant vice in most philosophers, and a happily married logician is almost a contradiction in terms. So many sages have regarded Woman as temptress because fornication often leads to marriage, which usually leads to children, which always leads to a respectable job and pretending to believe the idiocies your neighbors believe. The hypocrisy of the sages has been to conceal their timid onanism and call it celibacy.

It is very sad that the world has lost all interest in valuable things. Nowadays, if something is expensive people assume it must have value, which is like thinking a tedious job must be an important job.

Unless I have forgotten a few, I seem to have had affairs with twenty-three women during my wanderings after escaping the Priory. By the standards of my class and nation, this makes me nearly a virgin, and yet I dare to generalize about love. I think it is impossible to seduce a woman without being seduced by her. First, you think you want sex, then somehow she persuades you that you have fallen in love again, and finally you think you cannot live without her.

Dislike what I wrote yesterday; it shows a naivete I thought I had outgrown. No woman ever seduced me into thinking I was in love with her. I seduced myself. I am the type of idiot who falls in love easily.

Looking back over this notebook, I find the last sentence above to be the most intelligent thing I have written here. In fact, I may start a new game based on defining how many types of idiot I am.

I am the type of idiot who wants to write great music, even though nothing encourages me to think I have the talent. I am the type of idiot who wants to build an autokinoton—a self-moving carriage. I am the type of idiot who does not want to be Emperor of Europe even though a large conspiracy of astrologers and wizards believe that is my destiny and are willing to go to any lengths to help me arrive on the throne. I am the type of idiot who lives in a cabin far from civilization speculating on how many types of idiot I am. I am the type of idiot who lives in such a lonely cabin masturbating when experience has proven I am attractive enough to have all the mistresses I want. Oh, well, I am not the type of idiot who pretends that this flight from humanity is "celibacy" and "purity."

The cream of the jest: I am the type of idiot who is still in love with a myth called "Maria Maldonado," even though the real woman of that name is fourteen years older than the myth, no doubt has four or five children by now, and certainly does not look like, think like, or feel like the image of the Divine Girl in my mind.

My word, I just realized that Dante was the same sort of idiot as I am. In fact, he and I sing in poetry and music the same Platonic Archetype of the Divine Girl; we've just found different human females upon whom to attach the myth.

The secret of political and priestly power: Never realize what kind (or kinds) of idiot you are.

The secret of wisdom? Discover every type of idiot you are, *overlooking none*. The one you overlook is the one that will create your major disasters.

Honesty has destroyed more friendships than treachery. Never tell anybody anything "for his own good."

Opera is almost all about falling in love and very little about having to raise children. That may be why we prefer it to life, which is exactly the reverse.

A merchant buys things as cheaply as possible and sells them as expensively as possible, but the things have some worth or nobody would buy them. A priest sells nonexistent things and extorts every penny he can get. Therefore, the merchants are the more honorable profession. Q.E.D.

Why "is" music the greatest of the arts? Because I know more about it than I know about any of the other arts. Why "is" Napoli the most beautiful city in the world? Because I grew up there. Painting and Berlin will never be quite so important to me—but they are nonpareils to painters and Berliners. All emotions and ideas are equally relative. We feel and think what our history inclines us to feel and think.

I grow less human and more animal every day. That is, I am finally *more* and *less* than a Neapolitan musician.

Watching beavers build a dam yesterday, I was amused by the arguments I heard at the University of Paris about whether such behavior "is" intelligent or instinctual. I fear that that one little word "is" has driven all Europe mad.

The self or ego is a malign growth, virtually a cancer, caused by the society of other humans. I think it is contagious, and language may be the medium by which it infects each new generation.
The Mask is a morbid excrescence on the ego, and religion is the medium by which it infects all of us.

The apples grow on the apple tree without any central planning board, do they not? Sunset does not need an artistic director, does it? As the Magdalene gospel says, it is astounding that such great wealth has come here to live in poverty.

Better definition of ego than yesterday's: Ego is a social fiction for which one person at a time gets all the blame.

It is an atrocity to teach the Old Testament and European history to innocent children. Such knowledge can unhinge you if you're not old enough and tough enough to be reconciled to the fact that most men are criminal maniacs.

"Is," "is," "is"—the idiocy of the word haunts me. If it were abolished, human thought might begin to make sense. I don't know what anything "is"; I only know how it *seems to me at this moment*.

Yesterday I amused myself for a few hours by trying to "explain" a single blade of grass to my own satisfaction. I am flabbergasted that some professors I met in Napoli and Paris think they can explain something as complicated as a lobster—and that theologians try to explain the world itself.

Today I repeated again an old Priory experiment, staring at a blade of grass for an hour without trying to understand or explain it at all. The result was even more dumbfounding than my attempt to explain the grass fully. It became even more startling when I rediscovered suddenly, and experienced vividly, what Hume taught me years ago, namely that I was not seeing the grass at all but only mental picture of the grass constructed by my brain.

Nobody sees the obvious. Nobody observes the ordinary. There are more miracles in a square yard of earth than in all the fables of the Church.

I suddenly understand why my autokinoton has never worked. What I need to do is simply to create *controlled* explosions. Strange that it took me so long to see this. I knew that about my music all along.

There are worse things in life than my experiences

in the Bastille. For instance, trying to read an English novel.

A dog's dead body in the woods. The blood looks like human blood. I think: The clues are everywhere, but we do not see. Is it mere foppery that makes us think we are not animals, or is it that the noise & commotion of human society keep us from thinking clearly until we deliberately go into isolation?

I am beginning to believe my own Theory of the evolution of life—a bad sign. A man who believes his own Theory is almost a priest. Doubt all things, especially your own moments of illumination and insight.

I watch the ducks in the pond and observe how often they quarrel over space and territory. I presume this can be explained as an inbuilt reflex, but I also suspect the ducks enjoy it because it staves off boredom. Of course, if they could speak, they would no doubt explain these struggles in terms of Honor, Duty, and the Will of God. Fortunately, there are no journalists among the ducks, so the quarrels cease after everybody has had the fun of quacking and complaining for a few minutes, and has exercised their wing muscles in operatic gestures.

The wolves have their own politics, like the ducks. The "king" wolf can act just as haughty as any human monarch, but he seems much less oily and devious.

The earthworms have their own kind of society, I have observed. I begin to fear that politics is ubiquitous, which implies that stupidity is the quintessense of life.

* * *

Serious men are inevitably shallow, just as virtuous women are always dull. One must be a bit of a scoundrel to know the depths of one's self.

I was right to reject Vivaldi in my youth, when he was the fashion. Unless art is in constant revolution, it atrophies. Now that I begin to find my own voice, I can enjoy Vivaldi without becoming an echo of him.

I had just enough Jesuit education to make my honesty doubtful, even to myself.

Nobody has ever written an honest autobiography. Intuitively, we all understand that this is true and we know why it is true. Then we forget that theological and philosophical theories are all disguised autobiographies.

I must revise an earlier note: Politics is not ubiquitous. The trees exist in pure anarchy, Hobbesian war of all against all. We do not see this normally because their struggle is on a different time scale than animal life.

Nature, like music, has no immutable laws, only seasonal fashions. Animal politics (the clan, the clan leader, etc.) may be such a fad. The trees were here before us, and may be here after us.

It is impossible for me to believe that the human belly has the capacity to swallow all things or that the human brain can understand all things. Both physically and mentally, I am an animal who can digest so much and no more.

* * *

In the higher meditation states, I digest much, much more than usual, but I doubt that I truly digest "all." The mystics have never been self-critical or honest: These disciplines are the most precious inventions of our age of Reason.

Perhaps Weishaupt is right and the world badly needs one or two centuries of brutal materialism, to balance out the gibberish of the mystics and the hallucinations of the theologians. Then, perhaps, we will be able to meditate and learn something of value from the experience.

Nature has its own melody, harmony, and counterpoint, but the true joy of the wilderness is like that of music: not that "laws" are obeyed but that it is all so wonderfully useless.

In Nature and in music, "laws" are invented *after* the fact, to pretend to "explain"—actually, to obfuscate—what was done by spontaneity and the Will to Power.

If I understand them at all, Weishaupt and his cronies in the Illuminati wish to abolish Christianity by seizing power and then ordering everybody to become rational the next day after lunch. This is like trying to "cure" childhood by ordering all five-year-olds to become twenty-one immediately. Maturity takes a while for children and takes much longer for a species.

Everything now appears as play to me. I even suspect that "law" and "necessity" and "determinism" were invented by dull men in dusty reading rooms. "Natural Law" is the humbug of our century.

I begin to hear the sound of my own blood sometimes. I believe I will soon hear the sound of my hand moving in the empty air.

What every artist knows: No matter how beautiful the works of my contemporaries may be, I can find something wrong with them, if I try hard enough.

What every critic knows: Even those who cannot create can lift their legs and pee on the creators.

The birds sing to signal each other occasionally— another form of "language"—but mostly they sing for the joy of it, as I do.

Vivaldi: the Neopolitan heat, the Neopolitan eroticism, the Neopolitan paganism invading their "Christian" festivals.

Mozart: the planets revolving in Newtonian orbits, while children play and birds sing.

J.S. Bach: a naked goddess, a compass, a mason's square.

J. C. Bach: black opium in a lush and expensive brothel.

C.P.E. Bach: you see the loveliest woman in the world and then notice she has a nervous tic.

It has happened: I actually heard my hand move in the empty air. For hours afterwards, the grass was greener and the sky was bluer. This is not the merging of ego and world taught by the Craft; this is what the Eastern sages call Pure Mind.

Damn the fleas. If they did not exist I would still be a pantheist.

Low-flying geese at twilight: My heart soars with them. If I still believed in God all this beauty would be admirable but artificial. Precisely because I have lost God, I have found Pan.

Assuming for argument's sake that Christianity is true, I still would have had some helpful suggestions if I had been present at the Creation. If Papa Tetragrammaton had some divine reason for introducing a certain amount of fecal matter into our food, to poison some of us each generation, He still could have done it by means of creatures less annoying than the flies.

The mechanical picture of the universe, like the theological picture, is—just a picture. Existence is larger than any model that is not itself the exact size of existence (which has no size . . .)

If you can't offend part of your audience, there is no point in being an artist at all.

I cannot imagine the God of the Old Testament creating all this beauty. If He tried to make even a single oak leaf, He would bungle the job, go into a sulk and then rain brimstone on two towns and send plagues to five nations, just to express His childish petulance.

My autokinoton, once perfected, will not only travel without horses but fly above the rooftops. If I said that at the Royal Scientific Society they would want to put me in Bedlam.

I foresee that the worship of the appetites will some day have its priests and prophets, as the worship of intellect has today. Some century or other there may be a Holy War between the disciples of the God Rousseau and the cult of the Prophet Voltaire.

As far as I can calculate, scientific knowledge has doubled since about the time of Leonardo. This appears to be an accelerating differential function, so knowledge will double again before 1920. By then, my autokinotons will fly, even if I never find the way to build a working model. A later mechanic will succeed, if I fail. By 2020, autokinotons may even fly to the moon.

If anybody ever finds this diary, this is the page that will finally convince them I went mad alone here in the big woods.

If humanity is one being, as I discovered the morning I fought the duel with Carlo, it is also only one cell in the much bigger being that makes up the totality of life. Since the word "pantheism" hardly covers this thought, I must coin my own word. I think my present understanding can be called panvitalism. There is no governor anywhere but there are hierarchies of competing intelligences everywhere, all motivated by the joy of creativity and the Will to Power.

A diary is the only place you can discuss philosphy without immediately being placed under observation by the police.

If the big bisexual being called "Life" wants to escape this planet, then I must consider myself one of the specialized cells working on that project. My music speaks the urge, my clumsy autokinotons attempt to make the dream real. I ran away from the Priory because I cannot afford to waste time being an Emperor. I have more important work to do. I want to be the concert master for future evolution.

The song of the earth is perfect ecstasy. Only the individual mourns and complains.

The old Bach explains the universe better than Newton. No—change that. Johann Sebastian explains more than Newton to a mind like mine. I do not know what "is"; I only know what my mind can digest.

Anybody who has been to University knows how to debate with others. Only the wise know how to debate with themselves.

When you are totally alone the stars themselves are your companions.

If music is the greatest of the arts, as I like to think, why is it best understood by children and animals?

I am as unimportant to the ants as a man in China is unimportant to me. More: I can imagine the man in China. I doubt that the ants can imagine me.

Why does the sexual appetite cause so much unspeakable joy and irrational misery, so much suicidal and homicidal madness, and so much absurd theological ranting? Because every sexual choice is going to play a role in determining the temperament and talents of the next generation, and of all future generations who will inherit the earth from us. To be simple about it for once, a single friendly fuck can fill a continent with morons or geniuses in only a few thousand years.

Note on the above: All Jew-haters claim ''they'' are smarter than ''us.'' If there is any truth in this legend, it must be because the Jews never persuaded their brightest young men to enter monasteries and deposit their seed on lonely mattresses. Monasticism may have depopulated Europe of a few million possible Leonardos.

Sooner or later I will get the fleas out of the cabin; or I will give up and learn to live with the little bastards in my bed, my food, my clothes, my everything; or I will retreat back to civilization and they will have won. There is no negotiating with fleas.

The medicine-man, Miskasquamic, appeared to me again while I was meditating. He was just as solid and real as Uncle Pietro when he appeared to me in the dungeon where the Knights of Malta held me captive. I suspect he is the part of my mind that fears my own joy and freedom.

Medieval vanity: the desire to serve God.
Modern vanity: the desire to serve humanity.
''God'' and ''humanity'' may need me as much as I need fleas.

Science in the last century taught us to think for ourselves and believe our own observations against all the testimony of Authority. Science today increasingly tells us our thoughts and observations are reprehensible if they contradict its dogmas. The next two centuries may have to fight for the liberty of the individual mind against Science as the past two centuries had to fight against Theology.

The trees *know that I am here* just as surely as the wolves and bears do. I am not at all sure the ants know I am here, or would care if they did know.

I have been too hard on priests and lawyers in these notes. If they did not exist, there would be much less to laugh about in this world.

The mistake of the Deists: They recognize the God of the churches as a petulant tyrant: an enlarged image of the priests who invented that god. Then the Deists in turn imagine God as a mechanical inventor: an enlarged image of their own minds. The only "God" I can see in Nature is neither a moralist nor a rationalist. Its chief characteristic is an ardent passion for creating endless varieties of ugly little bugs.

Nature's God is inherently plural and at minimum two. The song of earth is a song of conflict, not resolution.

The whole of history is the refutation by experience of the doctrine that Nature's God has any morals or purposes that we can understand. To say that it has morals and purposes beyond our understanding may be consoling to the mournful and pacifying to the wrathful but contains no *meaning*. It is akin to the assertion that there may be a treasure buried in a cellar to which we can never gain access. Whatever "truth" there may be in an untestable proposition, it is irrelevant to who I am, where I am, and what is actually going on around me.

* * *

If turkeys could reason, they would doubt God because of the existence of hawks. If hawks could reason, they would doubt God because of the existence of men with arrows. If men with arrows could reason, they would never have invented God.

The young know everything. The mature doubt everything.

All laws are like Bavarian sausages: It is much easier to swallow them if you haven't seen how they are made.

The folly of the French atheists: They believe a universe without a monarch or a parliament—God or gods—is without intelligence. The apple seed knows all it needs to know to become an apple.

If all life is one, the fleas are my brothers? Yes, but often brothers cannot bear to live in the same house.

That note on the apple seed was oversimplified. It does not know "all" about how to become an apple; some of the "knowledge" is in the rain, the sun, the soil. Our one great error left over from Christian theology is to look for the monarch or First Cause of everything. It is hard to perceive what is right in front of our noses—that Chaos has its own rationality.

My "mind" is not in my head. It is partly in the history of the Latin-Italian tongues, partly in the history of other European languages I've mastered, partly in music, partly in books of philosophy and mechanics I have read.

Similarly, the theist and atheist both assume there is either a centralized "mind" somewhere ("God") or there is not. But the "mind" of existence is as decentralized as my "mind"—i.e. as the languages of Europe. It evolves as we evolve. It is not a noun but a verb, not a dancer but a dance. For clarity, this doctrine must never be called pantheism but panvitalism.

The Neopolitans dare not contradict their priests. The English dare not contradict their scientists. Mental slavery has its own fads and fashions.

The chief requisite for contentment is a bad memory.

I go back to Pure Mind more and more often. Yesterday it happened when a frog jumped into a pool. Today, when I heard the sound of my own hand clapping in the air again. It is nothing special in itself, and if it happens to an idiot, it just makes him a happier idiot. *Meditation is useless without trained skeptical observation of what is happening.*

Nature is without free will or determinism. There is exquisite and immediate adjustment, but no compulsion.

There is no "me" inside and no "God" outside. Pure Mind is pure Chaos, with 100 percent adjustment of each atom to the whole.

Try that last one again. "I" am as much outside as inside. The "world" is as much inside as outside. Euclidean geometry is fine for architects but does not include the data of psychology.

And one more attempt to say the same thing; the world is inside my head and my head is inside the world, and if those two propositions contradict each other in logic, they are still true in experience.

I kill to eat, like every other animal. I make music, like the birds. I shit on the ground, like the bears. Is there anything more marvelous than knowing this? I only go wrong when I start philosophizing and explaining.

Courage is a habit like any other. So is cowardice.

If everything in the world were useful and rational only the English would be happy.

Every sentence is an oversimplification, including this one. Every truth is a half-truth, including this one.

I can say all this so simply in music, but when I try to say it in words only paradox and nonsense approximate to what I mean.

Every clod of earth is part of the process that makes trees possible. Every tree is part of the process that made me possible. And I am part of a process that will make possible that which is so much greater than a human being that I cannot imagine it, except vaguely.

And yet, and yet, and yet—it is not a process. It is perfectly finished every second. All statements about it are relatively true, relatively false, and relatively nonsensical.

* * *

The whole earth itself is only one cell in the growing, dancing, evolving organism we call the galaxy.

Everything I have written has been as accurate and scientific as I could possibly make it, but it is only a record of what happens to consciousness when isolation is combined with deep meditation. The reality of the ordinary egotistic man in an ordinary city is just as "real" as what I am experiencing here.

There are no "delusions." All is truth to him or her who experiences it.

Carnivals are popular because they allow us to put Masks over our Masks.

The greatest discovery I have made in my whole life: If you don't instinctively want to tap your feet to it, it isn't good music. It's only rhetorical noise.

It is much easier to achieve Pure Mind here alone than it was at the Priory with Enlightened Masters teaching me. An Enlightened Master is ideal only if your goal is to become a Benighted Slave.

The "excluded middle" between Theism and Atheism—millions of rational minds in every atom, but no stasis anywhere. Chaos, in which every quantum of being is Will to Power.

Forms emerge from Chaos, linger awhile, fade away, and are replaced by new forms. This is absolutely all I know. Everything else is speculation—that is, acquired prejudices and wild guesses.

A great loneliness and a great forgiveness are battling to capture my heart and tear me away from my freedom. It is easy to love humanity, after all—if there are none of the sons of bitches within a thousand miles.

Shall I summarize what I have learned in my loneliness and freedom? The web of life is a beautiful and meaningless dance. The web of life is a process with a moving goal. The web of life is a perfectly finished work of art right where I am sitting now.

These propositions cannot all be true in logic, but they are true nonetheless. So much the worse for logic.

The web of life is also a seamless unity (I and the bear are brothers) and parts of the unity are at war with other parts. Chaos prevails over all, in perfect harmony.

Snow falls and trees turn white. Winter comes without any accountants or committees planning the shape of each snowflake.

I think I am becoming a moron. I understand nothing. I stare in wonderment at everything.

The Bible assures us there is fear in a handful of dust. Typical religious mania. There is infinite ecstasy in a handful of dust. The stupidest error of the Rationalists: their concept of "inanimate matter." The energy of stars and the life of all beings are in every atom.

We can only think about what we can talk about. Thinking is talking to ourselves. Where the words are missing, we must perforce write music or speak in jokes and parables.

* * *

Intellectual laziness and common sense are the same thing. Common sense is just the trade name of the firm.

The greatest folly of all is to think that this moment can be other than it is. The second greatest folly is to blame oneself for the moment being what it is. The third greatest folly is to find somebody else to blame.

The first folly is called Imagination, the second Conscience, and the third, Improving the World. These follies are all perversions of language, based on comparing what we can think about with what we actually encounter and endure.

It is these perversions of language that have made us human and may yet make us more than human. If we were totally sane, we would never think of anything but what we actually encounter and endure, like the other animals.

Animals show all the human emotions *but only in the present tense.* They do not brood over the past or worry about the future, because they have no language for events not present in perception at the instant. This is why they are happier and less creative than humans.

I must burn these pages when I leave here. God forbid that anybody ever find them. "Panvitalism" might become a new religion, and I would be the first heretic burned for arguing that it's only a theory, not a proven truth.

The Will to Power was an exhilarating concept when I thought of it, but now I see that it is just another explanation created after the fact, to account for *what is the only possible resultant of all the vectors and trajectories in the web of Chaos.* I was closer to the mark when I said all is play.

I foresee a possibility worse than a new Church of Panvitalism, which will only happen if theologians take up my ideas. If the present Gentleman's Club of Science comes on the idea of the unity of life, they will convert it into the doctrine of Pan-Mechanism.

To talk at all is to lie either (a) for politeness or (b) because of vanity or (c) for more reprehensible motives, i.e. fraud and treachery or (d) because language cannot contain our deepest experiences and insights. The longer one is silent, the more easy it is to stop lying even to oneself and see behind the Masks of conventionality.

Behind the Mask of politics and priestcraft: the Will to Power.

Behind the Mask of the Will to Power: the ecstasy of the dance, the joy of meaningless play.

Behind the Mask of dance and play: Chaos and the void.

Behind the Mask of Chaos and the void: my simple mind trying to explain the impressions that impinge upon me.

You are precisely as big as what you love and precisely as small as what you allow to annoy you.

Gunshots a long, long way off. At first I thought they were rumbles of thunder. No, it is just idiots making History.

The loneliness assaults me again. Ah, for the conversation of intelligent men and women—the love of women—the special love of one woman—and being a father might be a most educational experience. The voice of temptation tells me I am not meant to be a sage but a participant.

Turkey tracks in the snow. In one moment this simple vision proved and refuted all my theorizing. Turkey tracks in the snow, and no Law determined which directions and turns the bird took. A goose honks in the distance, then a wolf howls.

Turkey tracks in the snow: the bird walks now this way, now another way.
I am near the end of what words can say.

This is the truth, this is the truth, this is the truth:
turkey tracks in the snow
fleas in my clothes
I am cold and hungry
It all coheres

8. My Lady Greensleeves

Lousewortshire 1777

52 cards in 4 suits,
52 weeks in 4 seasons

As it pleased our Lady, Maria Babcock became a Witch, as she had become a Revolutionary, without any inner Conflict about so Momentous a step, for the Law of the Great Work is Necessity, not Chance, and the Path is laid down in each case for the One who must needs walk upon it; yea for the One who must needs walk upon it.

DE CAECITIA HOMINUM

Know then that Maria's closest Confidant in Lousewartshire, ever since the birth of her first Child, had been Old Kyte, the town's Midwife and Herbalist, and everybody knew Kyte was a Witch. But this was the Age of Reason, so nobody believed Kyte put Curses on Cows or Flew through the Air on a Broomstick; they just thought the Aged Crone was "superstitious" and a bit old-fangled. Even people who used Kyte's Herbs when the doctor's Medicines failed to help them did not think there was anything Wicked or Eldritch about the old lady, and certainly they did not think the herbs were Magickal—it was just that some of the Herbs worked sometimes.

Maria knew that Old Kyte had secret & es .eric Knowledge of more than herbal healing; yea, of Arts Arcane and Recondite. After the birth of Ursula—when Kyte had arrived "by coincidence" when Dr. Coali was unavailable—Maria had insisted on being attended by Kyte during her next two Labours, when Maria Anne and little Johnny were born. The old Midwife knew more about "Women's Mysteries," as she called her Specialty, than Dr. Coali or any ten Physicians in the County. In fact, she thought women's Problems should be treated by women Physicians, and once told Maria that someday, in the Future, women like herself would be admitted to Medical schools and allowed to become Physicians.

Maria told her that would only happen when the World through Waxing of Wisdom and Waning of Folly no longer believed it required a Willy to practise the Art of Medicine scientifically. The old woman laughed delightedly and said, "You are a rare 'un, my lady."

DE PERICULO JOCORUM AMORIS

And so it was quite Natural, one day when Old Kyte had dropped by to offer Advice on Johnny's Teething problems, for Maria to ask her directly what she would never ask a Male physician.

"Without rejecting my husband, whom I love," she enquired, "is there some secret in your lore by which I can avoid the usual Disaster of becoming pregnant every year until I drop of Exhaustion?"

"Aye," Kyte said. "I was a-wonderin' what year you'd be askin' that."

"And will you tell me?"

"That I shall, my lady, an' you be as brave as I suspeck. Tis a secret of the craft."

All Maria knew about "the Craft" was that Kyte used it in childbirthing. It involved Common Sense, Intuition, a great deal of Love, and some mysterious Entities or Elementals, visible only to Kyte, called Robin, Marion, Orfee, and Bride. "And how may one learn the secrets of the Craft?" she asked directly.

"By initiation, my lady." The old woman watched Maria carefully then. "An' a lass ha'e heart, she may learn the Art."

Maria knew that John had gone through several initiations to learn the Secrets of Freemasonry, whatever they were. Such Occult societies were still quite normal, even in the Age of Reason. At the same time, Maria knew that, less than a Century ago, she and Old Kyte could both have been Burned for what they were Discussing, for such was the Blindness and Bigotry of the Black Brothers of those days. In Napoli, where the Inquisition survived, burnings were still theoretically Possible, although the last had been many years ago.

She asked simply, "When can I be initiated?"

DE LIBRA, IN QUA QUATTUOR VIRTUTES AEQUIPOLLENT

Maria was initiated on May 1, 1777, which was one of the "Quarter Days," according to Kyte. The other Quarter Days were midsummer, Halloween, and midwinter, and each Quarter Day was an "Opening of the Gate" to one of the "guardians"—Robin, Marion, Orfee, or Bride. Two of the guardians were Male and two Female, Old Kyte explained in advance, because the Craft was concerned with Balancing Energies, this being the most Antient Secret of the Art Magickal.

The four Seasons, the four Guardians, the four Suits of the Tarot deck, the four "elements" of Alchemy, all contained the same Symbolic Language, and all intuitive persons understand some of it, but Kyte said even the Wisest could study all her life and not understand the Whole of it. These Balances, quoth she, be stronger than Thought, for they be the Conditions and Preconditions of Mind itself & the Bedrock of the Will which is Steersman and Navigator to Life, Love, and Liberty; yea, Steersman and Navigator to Life, Love, and Liberty. Amen.

The initiation took place in the woods north of Lousewartshire, and in May the nights are still sore chilly with hoarfrost in merry England. Maria thought wryly that the Freemasons were smarter than the Witches in one way: They held their Initiations indoors and avoided the pest, Frostbite; yea, they held their Initiations indoors and avoided the pest, Frostbite.

She was Blindfolded and spoke to each of the Guardians in turn, as she was led in a Species of Inward-turning Spiral Dance. Of course, the Guardians were Personated by human members of Old Kyte's Study-group or Coven or whatever this was called. Each had a Formula of Power for Maria, and the Formulae were: "Have Brain enough to Know," "Have Belly enough to Dare," "Have Heart enough to Will," and, finally, "Have Common Sense enough to Keep Silence." Give Ear, Give Ear most Earnestly, all ye who may someday Tred the Path of the Moon and enter the Gate of the Rose Ruby and the White Gold to the Palace of Felicity for there be Herein Four Rules with Four Meanings Each and Wisdom alone availeth to find the Four Applications of each Meaning.

Then Maria had the Blindfold removed and was alone with Greensleeves.

Everybody else had Vanished—probably Hiding behind trees.

DE FORMULAE FEMINAE

This, Maria knew, went back to what Old Kyte called "the burning time." If Maria were a Church Spy, or changed her Mind about wishing to be a member of the Craft, she could not identify anybody except the one who had Dared bring her here, Old Kyte herself, for such be the Rule of the Craft to hele all, an' it please Our Lady.

Greensleeves was a Goddess most Beautiful & most Sublime, dressed only in Leaves and early Spring Flowers, most fragrant, and the Leaves were the richest Green and the Flowers were the brightest of Blues and Reds and Yellows, like rare Jewels, yea like rare Jewels. And in sooth Greensleeves looked a great Deal like Kyte, as a matter of Fact, but seemed at least forty years younger and had none of the old woman's personal Traits in Posture or Expression of the face or even in Language. She spoke almost without accent and almost without Human intonation.

Old Kyte was being *possessed* by Greensleeves.

She told Maria that they had Met Before, many Times, in many Ages, and that Maria had been Initiated in this way in many Lifetimes. She said that Maria would never Once in her Life regret the choice she made when returning once more to the Craft of the Old Times, yea to the Craft of the Old Times.

Then she ordered Maria to Lie on the Ground, face down, and learn to Know the Energy of Spring, the elemental Force called Robin and the Knight of Wands, the alchemical Fire that warms the Cosmic Furnace.

Yea, and verily She warned Maria most Vehemently and Ominously not to Rise until she was Summoned.

After that, the very Minutes were like empty hours. Maria, in Spite of her Trust in Old Kyte, and the great Love she bore toward her, began to have waves of Doubt and agenbite of Anxiety. She worried that Ugly Things might Crawl under her Clothes and bite her, and that Loathesome and Slimy Things might Sore Afflict her. She began to resent all this Ritual Mystification. She felt Chilly and Damp and thought a Head Cold or Pernicious Influenza might result from this archaic & druidic nonsense.

Then she remembered the Healing Power in her hands and began to use it.

The Earth became Warm and Safe again. Nothing would harm her. Instead, all the Living Things and tiny Creatures of Our Lady growing or living in the soil began to Resonate with Maria's Healing Rays and feed warmth back to her. She understood what the Knight of Wands symbolizes, and why Alchemical "fire" is not ordinary fire. She realized why the Quarter days are important, and how Eros and Reproduction and the Four Seasons are Marks on a Cosmic Clock, ticking the Seconds of vast Eternity. She began to feel the Joy that had raised her to the Stars, yea to the Stars, when first hearing Mr. Handel's "Messiah" oratorio.

"For He is like a refiner's fire."

"Cum' along now. No sense gettin' a chill, my lady." It was the Voice of Kyte again, in her own speech. "Greensleeves" had gone back to what Kyte called "Side," which was where the elementals live when not Summoned forth by the Craft. Side was part of the Mind, in a sense, but not the individual Mind of one Woman, or one Man, but the Mind that was and is and shall be in all Permutations of Consciousness in all Entities soever, be they past or be they present or be they Yet to Become.

Old Kyte led Maria back to her own Cottage, made Tea, and taught her the first Secret of the Craft: a Sponge well Soaked in Vinegar, inserted in the Vagina, before the Sports and Games of a Night of loving, then leave it in all ye Night and only Remove it in the Morning, after Sir Chaunticleer, the Lord of the Chicken Run, doth Raise his Voice to Crow. And thrice repeat the rhyme:

> I love the bairns that I do ha'e
> But one more bairn could mean my gra'e
> Greensleeves, be with me!
> Pax Sax Serax!

DE LUDO AMORIS

In the following Year, Maria Practised this antient Contraception and did not become Pregnant again. Meanwhile, she underwent three further intiations, at the three remaining Quarter Days, and learned that the Craft contained a great deal of Superstition, and equal Amount of uncommon Common Sense, much Gynecological Knowledge unknown or little-known to the all-male Medical Profession, so Proud of their wonderful Willies that they never Thought to ask a Woman's Opinion of Feminine Matters, and an intricate System of seasonal Symbolism that increasingly seemed to make sense in a way that was midway between Mathematics and Poetry.

Robin, the Fiery Dionysian energy of Spring, Maria had come to understand, was a spirit from the Dawn of Consciousness when the Willy first became Holy.

So was Orfee, the Airy autumnal energy of the practical Arts and pure Sciences. But these Solar and Phallic forces were "balanced" as Kyte said by Lunar and Female forces—the Watery summer energies of Marion and the Earthy winter energies of Bride. Male, female, male, female: a four-part Wheel turning in an Infinite Circle, yea in an Infinite Circle.

On May Eve, 1798, Maria had been in the Craft one year, and Old Kyte presented her with a White cord. To learn the more advanced Secrets of the Craft, and earn a Red cord, and the Right to wear the Garter of a Priestess, Maria would have to Master the technique of *becoming*, not just talking to, Our Lady Greensleeves; for in the Craft, although the Willy be honored as All-Father and Sol Invictus, the Light Absolute, the Womb of Creation is honored equally as Earth Mother and Starry Furnace of Creation; and Possession of a Willy is not considered Necessary in Order to Communicate and obtain the Knowledge and Conversation of the Divine.

Maria had already learned, by then, that by Vivid Visualization her healing Power could be altered into the Capacity to "melt" into and merge somewhat with Aspects of the seasonal Energies. She had, to a certain degree, merged with Robin and Marion and Orphee and Bride and found Fiery and Watery and Airy and Earthy parts of herself that were Mirrors of similar forces in Nature, the Greatest being always contained within the Smallest and the Cosmic Whole in Every Part. She understood that it was by Bringing all these Together, making a Psychic Pyramid of four Equal Sides, that she could melt and merge and become One with Greensleeves, who was a Mortal woman and an Aeon and a Goddess and a symbol of earth all at once.

For six months Maria worked on Knowing and Daring and Willing and Keeping Silence, as she learned how to melt and merge with Greensleeves.

At the Sabaat on Halloween, she succeeded. It happened as the Spiral Dance reached its center, representing Winter and Death, and began to unwind again toward Spring and Rebirth. Coming out of the center, the Focus, Maria almost Fainted, and then felt herself Glowing with a New and indescribable Energy, as if Fire and Water were one, yea as if Fire and Water were one.

All the pain of her three Childbirths came back at once, and all the Joy of the Deliveries at the end of the Pain, and the two merged, so she was Pushing down to end the pain and feeling the Babe come out of her, again and again and again, Pain and Ecstasy mingling in an Infinite Circle from the Beginning of Time to the End, which was a new Beginning, and all that existed was Pain and Ecstasy and Infinity: Pain and Ecstasy *meeting* in Infinity. She was all the Women who had ever birthed a Child, and she was all the female Animals, too, and she was the Earth itself bringing forth spring out of the Death and Darkness, yea and verily, out of the Death and Darkness.

And then she saw Sigismundo Celine, the mad Musician and Punchinello who had shot her Brother, Carlo, in a stupid masculine Duel, and a Red Indian with him. They were looking Startled, and sore Amazed, as if they had not Expected to see her.

And then she saw Soldiers shivering in a cold Valley, badly Clothed, without Hope, waiting for the enemy to find them and end their Miserable lives, yea a Multitude of Soldiers in a cold Valley.

And she saw that James Moon, who had once worked as a Coachman at Babcock Manor, was among these pitiful Dying men, and he doubted all the Gods and all the Hopes of those who had been spared the Valley in the Cold Winter which he endured.

And she saw John carrying a pure & pearly white Stone with the four words *Et in Arcadia Ego* on it, and there were four Guardians at the four Quarters, called Worshipful Masters, and John was undergoing the same initiation as herself, in only a slightly different Form.

And the Light covered her, and the Light *sang*, verily in troth the Light *sang:* and the Light shone in Darkness, and the Darkness knew it Not.

DE OPERIBUS STELLAE MICROCOSMI QUORUM SUNT QUATTUOR MAJORES

It was a few Nights later that Maria Discovered the first French translation of *I Ching* in the family Library. John must have Purchased it recently, without mentioning that he had Acquired such a Curiosity.

Maria had heard somewhere that the *Ching* was supposed to be the Oldest Book in the World. She opened it and started Browsing.

John, she discovered, had been Browsing before her. Next to each of the sixty-four hexagrams, he had written a Peculiar kind of Number. Maria stored at John's Numbers a long time without recognizing them.

```
000000
000001
000010
000011
000100
```

—and so on, to 111111. Maria's education had not
included Leibniz's Binary notation, so this was far
from Clear to her, but she recognized, eventually, that
each Number was Isomorphic to the Chinese Hexagram beside which John had scrawled it. He had simply replaced the *I Ching* solid Yang lines with *1*'s and
the broken Yin lines with *0*'s.

Maria turned to the Back of the Book. There John
had made a final Notation that said, to her Astonish-
ment,

$$Y = 01 = \text{fire}$$
$$H = 00 = \text{water}$$
$$V = 11 = \text{air}$$
$$H = 10 = \text{earth}$$

In a flash, Maria "understood"—and then Realized
she understood Nothing. But it was Clear that John
was working, for his own Reasons, on the Mathematical symbolism she had intuited underlying Witchcraft, and he had found it, somehow, in the Yins and
Yangs of this antient Chinese book, yea the oldest
Book in the World.

Mother Ursula had neglected Cabalistic exegesis,
along with Binary notation, in Maria's education, but
Maria knew enough Bible lore to Recognize that
YHVH was the Holy Unspeakable Name of God. John
was somehow relating Jewish Mysticism to both Chinese Philosophy and Alchemy. He had hit on the Symbolism of the Craft without knowing the Craft. Then
she remembered:

"*. . . for the Widow's son . . .*" John was saying.

". . . brothers in the Craft . . ." somebody was answering.

Was that in Napoli or here in England?

Phrases that Maria had heard Years ago suddenly came back to her. She had seen her Father, Count Maldonado, and John exchange a certain Strange Handshake home in Napoli that John usually reserved for other Whigs here in England. Was it Charles Putney Drake in London or his cousin Robert Drake in Napoli who also exchanged that Handshake with John once and muttered those Cryptic Words that seemed to be about Parcifal, the son of the poor Widow, the pure Fool who found the Holy Grail? And how could she have forgotten that John and a Friend spoke of "the Craft" on that occasion—years before she had heard Old Kyte use that Expression?

Maria thought of Freemasonry.

She had known for a Long Time that John was a Freemason.

It was Amusing, even if part of her was a little Frightened. The two Things that were Denounced by the priests in Napoli most often in her Girlhood had been Witchcraft and Freemasonry; and now she was a Witch and married to a Freemason.

Then she thought two things at once: *My God, is freemasonry the male form of witchcraft?* and, humorously, They *might think witchcraft is the female form of freemasonry.*

DE ARCANO NEFANDO

Sir John Babcock, by then, was thirty-three years old and Generally regarded as the Handsomest and

Craziest man in Parliament. He Secretly enjoyed both Reputations, but also secretly Believed he was the worst Scoundrel in Parliament and that the next time a Blazing Rock fell out of the Sky it might hit him Square on the Cranium, yea Square on the Cranium, as a Punishment for his Iniquities.

He loved Maria and their three children with a Constant and sincere Devotion; indeed, his friend Edmund Burke once said that John was the most Loving Husband and Father in all England. His single problem was that, not so Constantly or Sincerely as he loved Maria, but often enough to drive him to occasional Bouts of Blind Drunkenness to stave off Temptation, he also loved certain Boys of about eighteen who had a brutal Manly beauty about them.

He had been Blackmailed once, by an Irish coachman named Moon, and since then had Learned to be even more Careful. That did not really help, psychologially: The acts that he wished to think of as Prudence oft seemed mere Duplicity and made him feel more like a Sneaking Villain.

Naturally, the more this Guilt afflicted him, the harder he drove himself to work for any and every Humanitarian cause.

As he had advanced through the degrees of Freemasonry, his mind had expanded increasingly from the Political to the Abstract and philosophical. Basically, he saw every Religion as a Crude, often Crazed, Fragment of a great System of psychology that had somehow survived, relatively undebased, in the Rituals of the Free and Accepted Craft. This system of psychology used Alchemical and Cabalistic symbols, but— unlike formal Religion—taught the Practatus gradually to see beyond the symbols to the eternal Human Constants they represented.

He had made a great Discovery when looking into an old Chinese book he had bought out of idle Curiosity. He had Communicated this to some Fellows of the Craft in London and they were greatly Amaz'd and much excited, also.

John remembered—how could he ever forget?—the night Ursula was born, when Old Kyte had Spoken unguardedly of "the Craft." He had wondered since then, off and on, if the Folk-religion that Kyte practised, which people called "Witchcraft," might have had some Historical connection, long ago, with Freemasonry—why else would the term "the Craft" have survived in both Traditions?

DE ARTE AMORIS ET DELICARIUM MYSTICI

One night, when he least Expected it—right after they had enjoyed the Sport and Holy Ritual of Love, in fact—Maria casually asked him about the *I Ching*. Women have a singular Gift, he thought, for asking Questions you don't want to answer just when you are in the Mood to deny them Nothing, yea, when you are in the Mood to deny them Nothing.

"I was interested in *I Ching* because of the amazing coincidence of the notation being similar to Leibniz's binary numbers," he explained sleepily. "Besides, some people claim it's the oldest book in the world."

"What are binary numbers?"

John explained how, using only two Symbols, every number could be represented as Combinations of these two. "Leibniz used 1 and 0. The *I Ching* used the straight lines called 'yang' and the broken lines called 'yin,' but the two systems are isomorphic. It would be the same if you used a circle and a square, or a question mark and an exclamation point. Any two symbols will do the job.''

"I was looking at the book and I saw the notes you made," Maria said, yawning. "It makes sense now. You turned every hexagram into a binary number. It certainly is astonishing how the two systems fit each other.''

"It astonished Leibniz," John said, sitting up and pouring some Wine into a Glass. "He saw this translation of the *I Ching* when it appeared in France and it knocked him off his pins, I've read. Want some?" At her nod, he poured another glass. "His whole philosophy of monadology is an attempt to explain, really, why such coincidences are possible. You have such a gift for happy coincidences you must have thought about that, haven't you?''

"The part contains the whole," Maria said. "Leibniz never expressed it that way, but that is the only way I can understand it.''

John stared at her. "Those are approximately the words I have found, myself, in groping to understand this perplexity. The binary system was in the minds of some ancient Chinese sages thousands of years ago and in Leibniz's mind fifty or sixty years ago because it is buried somehow in every mind. The implications are staggering. As Leibniz said, there may be a cosmic Logical Language within each of us, lying virtually untapped.''

They sipped their Wine and then John rose to Stoke the Fire up a bit.

"What did you have in mind in those notes at the end?" Maria asked. "I could see that you were equating the letters in the Hebrew name of God with the four elements. How does that associate with the binary numbers or *I Ching*?''

John climbed back into her Bed and Snuggled closer
for Warmth, it being a Typically Wretched English
Night. He thought a moment. "You know I am a Freemason," he said finally. "I do not believe the oaths
of secrecy are any more than nonsense at this stage of
history—they date back to the times when the Inquisition existed everywhere. Still, I have taken the oaths,
and they are binding. Forgive me if I speak somewhat
guardedly. Part of Speculative Masonry—I can tell you
this much—deals with the four 'souls' within each of
us, or the four parts of each human mind, or perhaps
it is only four levels of organization in our brains.
These are symbolized by—"

"Fire, water, air, and earth," Maria said. "And
the four letters in the name of God—aren't they *yod,
hay, vauf, hay?*—also symbolize these four parts of
each of us. Is your oath broken if I guess correctly,
sir?"

John hugged her. "You never cease to amaze me,"
he said. "If I didn't know better, I'd swear you had
hidden under the table at a Freemasonic lodge. How
did you do it?"

"The way you related all this to *I Ching,*" Maria
said. "A kind of intuitive logic of the symbolism. Because it is in all of our minds latently, as you said."

"It is in Celtic art, too," John said. "In Trinity
College in Dublin, where I grew up, is a book over a
thousand years old. It's called the Book of Kells because it was created by monks in a monastery near
Kells. Over and over the same four symbols appear in
it—a lion, a man, an eagle, and a bull. Are you as
clever as I think, *cara mia?*"

Maria only had to ponder a few moments. "Leo is
a fire sign. The lion, Leo, is fire, then. The man must
be Libra, water. The eagle is Aquarius, air. Taurus,

the bull, is an earth sign. So, once again, the code is fire, water, air, and earth.'' She smiled. ''And astrology is a heresy to the Church. I suppose nobody told those Irish monks about that.''

''The monks would have replied that they were not astrologers at all. The symbolism comes from Ezekiel in the Old Testament. He saw an angel with four faces—lion, man, eagle, bull.''

''Lion, man, eagle, bull,'' Maria repeated thoughtfully. ''Fire, water, air, and earth. Wands, cups, swords, and discs in the Tarot. And in the ordinary playing cards, clubs, hearts, spades, and diamonds.''

She was thinking, but not speaking, of Robin, Mariah, Orfee, Bride. John was thinking, but not speaking, of the Worshipful Masters of the North, East, South, and West in Masonic ceremony.

''Fifty-two cards in four suits,'' John said finally. ''Fifty-two weeks in four seasons. It is a collective symbolism in all our minds, and the makers of calendars used it, too.''

''And what is your hand doing there, sir?''

''Gentle, stimulating afterplay. Recommended in Dr. Tenero's book of instruction for young bridegrooms.''

''Indeed, sir! Dr. Tenero is a saucy rogue. But what were those notes you wrote at the end of *I Ching?*''

''The symbols for active yang, passive yang, active yin, and passive yin. I converted them into binary, as I was converting the whole book into binary.''

''You might move your hand a bit more, but gently, darling. Gently. Ah, yes. Those are the same four psychic forces again? The Chinese equivalents of fire, water, air, and earth?''

''Yes. But because they are more abstract, they are

more general. Nobody can take them too literally, as some seem to have taken the four elements too literally in early chemistry. Oh, yes, darling. Just rub it slightly, like that. Just a little. For a few moments.''

"What do you think it all means, John?"

"There is a collective psychology of the species, as I just said, and it is deeper than our individual psychology. There is one mind, and we are all aspects of it. Or something like that. Oh, *cara mia, cara mia.*"

"*Caro mio.* So huge, so fast. Like magic. That must be how the Willy originally came to be worshipped. It is impossible you can be ready so soon, is it not?"

"With faith in the Lord all is possible."

"You mean . . . ?"

"Perhaps in a few moments."

"Active and passive yang are both male," Maria said thoughtfully. "Active and passive yin are both female. That symbolism is not explicit in the fire-water-air-earth tradition."

"But it is in the Tarot cards you just mentioned."

"Oh, yes. Is this your wand or your sword, sir?"

"It's the wand now, because active. The sword is passive and intellectual. Dissection and analysis. And is this your cup or your disc?"

"The cup. Very active. I would say, very damned active, sir, if I were not a lady of refinement and breeding."

"My God in Heaven!" John cried suddenly.

"Are you about to . . ."

"No, not yet, but almost. I just realized . . . here, let me shift over . . . like this . . ." He Entered her Gently, and she felt the Alchemical Fire in the Cosmic Furnace begin again.

"*Caro mio.*"

"I just realized . . . oh, darling . . . it's in the Grail legend, too."

"Parcifal's lance that redeems the wasteland . . ."

"Yes."

"And a good lance it is tonight, too. Ah, God, God."

"And a sweet Grail, too, full of all the, all the, God, all the treasures of the, of the . . ."

"Oh, darling. Darling John."

In the Afterglow, Maria was thinking, not-thinking, of other Nights of lovemaking and of her childbirths and the Secrets Kyte taught and the music she Loved, especially Mozart, and then she was thinking clearly again and said, "John, I think I should tell you. I belong to, well, you might call it a women's study group . . ."

TENEBO, ILLEGITIMATI: PERDURABO

But John was already soundly Asleep and beginning to Snore and Snort and Gasp as a man will when he has had Enough of the Sports of Love, and then he became Silent as one who has Tasted the Ambrosia of Paradise, yea Silent as one who has Tasted the Ambrosia of Paradise.

But Maria was thinking of the thirteen in each Wiccan Coven and the thirteen cards in each of the four suits, the thirteen Weeks in each of the four Seasons, Vivaldi's *Four Seasons* music running through her head, and the thirteen at the Last Supper, and the sun, which is One, moving in eternal circle through the twelve Houses, one plus twelve being thirteen, and why did the Order of the Garter have one hundred sixty-nine or thirteen times thirteen members? And if all this could be coded, as John said Leibniz said, into the one and the zero, the upright 1 and the cauldron-like zero, the wand and the cup, one l'oeuf one vier, on love on wir, ein loaf ein vir, and she sloped down and slooped up and slipped round into sleep.

9. Cherry Valley

Space–time and beyond

We don't got to show you no steeenking reality

Cherry Valley is a beautiful name. It sounds like Spring and fresh growing things and sunlight and roosters crowing and larks singing and, of course, cherry blossoms as delicate as those painted by the Zen artists of Japan. Cherry Valley is the kind of name that makes you think that you should go there and see for yourself how beautiful Nature can be.

There was nothing beautiful about Cherry Valley, New York, when Colonel Seamus Muadhen entered it in November 1778.

Seamus had been sent down to Cherry Valley with five medical officers and a small troop to give the survivors what assistance was possible and to protect the medics in case the Loyalists returned. He had heard about what had happened in Cherry Valley and knew the carnage would be terrible to see, but after two years of war, he thought he had confronted enough blood and horror to have a strong enough belly for anything.

The Loyalists were sincere patriots who loved their king and firmly believed God was on their side. They regarded Jefferson as a madman, the Declaration of Independence as treason, and General Washington as

Satan incarnate. Together with Indian allies they had set out to make an example of Cherry Valley, to warn other communities what could happen to those who gave aid and shelter to the demonic rebel army. The Loyalists meant well, or at least they meant something.

From a distance, Seamus already knew it would be worse than he expected. There was hardly a house left standing. Every living creature that had not been shot or bayoneted to death must have died in the burning, he thought. There would be precious little work for the medical staff.

"Christ," he said. "We should have brought undertakers instead of doctors." But, although he was disgusted and saddened again, as he often was by the scenes of warfare, his guts and nerves were not overreacting: Two years of battle had made him tough. He was sure he could deal with whatever pitiful sights Cherry Valley contained.

But then as he and his men approached closer, they began to hear a few wailing, keening sounds. Some people, or animals, in Cherry Valley were still alive, or half-alive.

They sounded like wounded cats at first.

One day while they were sitting together listening to the hot yellow brook bubble, the Reverser told Miskasquamish a story.

Across the great water, the Reverser said, there were men of medicine who once made mighty tipis. These were bigger and grander than his own square tipi, and they were made of rich veined stone instead of wood, and the men of medicine who created these wonders were called Free Builders. These Free Builders studied many secrets of medicine and were more ambitious than Miskasquamish. They wished to cure not just suffering individuals but the entire suffering race of humanity. It was their aim to help all human beings walk through the gate of the four quarters and become like gods.

Then, the Reverser said, there was a quarrel among the Builders and they became two instead of one. They have been fighting ever since, and the two became three and four, as new differences arose. The fight goes on, and it is called "history," and most people are its victims and do not even know what the fight is about.

There was one man, the Reverser said, who tried to stop all the fighting. He knew that the men of medicine were all sick now from the bad medicines that anger made in their bodies, and he tried to sober them up. He tried very hard. He was very kind and patient, and he never stopped trying. They killed him by nailing him to a cross and hanging him up in the hot afternoon sunlight in summer to die slowly.

Miskasquamish thought about that story, while they sat and listened to the brook and the singing birds. The brook was yellow, Miskasquamish had once explained, because it has an earth spirit in it. The Reverser, just to be contrary, said the brook was yellow because it had a kind of substance called "sulphur" in it.

"That man in the story was your father," Miskasquamish said finally.

"No. But that was a good guess. The father of my tribe, you might say."

Miskasquamish said then, "Every Reverser has his reasons for reversing the laws. Some are bitter from the unfairness of the world. Some have been hurt so much they are broken inside and cannot think clearly anymore. Some are mastered by anger. In every case, there is a reason of some kind. I know that, so I do not judge or condemn. But where the Reverser goes, he makes reversals, and the world does not work, and things fall apart.''

The Reverser arose and walked to the magic water place. He pulled down one rope and the other rope came up with water in a bucket. He drank and offered it.

Miskasquamish had seen that magic so often that it no longer disturbed him. He drank without fear.

"It took me five moons to build this wooden tipi," the Reverser said then. "It was hard work. I thought I would have a place where I would not have to argue with Builders anymore or defend myself against their magic."

Miskasquamish thought about that. "Nobody has asked you to move away," he said carefully.

"I think I have an ordinary nose," the Reverser said. "But if a man of medicine came to me many times and talked about long noses, and if such a man of medicine led the speech back to long noses, no matter what the topic had been before, so all talk always circled back to long noses, after a while I would begin to think that either I had a very, very long nose or else the man of medicine was obsessed with long noses in general."

Miskasquamish said reasonably, "But we were not talking about long noses."

"I have given you furs. I have fed you on turkey and berries. I have shared my water with you. I have acted with respect."

"Reversers do many good things, just to reverse our expectations of what Reversers do."

The Reverser said something in his own tongue. It

sounded like *mor taycreesto*. He stood up and walked to the wooden tipi and came out with a long metal stick. He pointed the stick at a nearby tree. There was a sudden shocking roar of thunder. A branch fell off the tree. The Reverser looked cold and unfriendly and turned to show his anger to Miskasquamish. Then he pointed his metal stick at another tree a long way across the clearing. There was roaring thunder again. A bird fell out of the tree.

"Five moons I worked on this tipi," the Reverser said. "Hard work. The tipi is mine. I will stay here."

"Nobody asked you to go away," Miskasquamish said, keeping his face quiet and ignoring the sweat that poured out of him since the stick made thunder the second time and the bird died far away across the clearing where the stick was pointing. But he stood up then.

"Perhaps we will meet another day," he said courteously.

"I somehow feel sure of it," the Reverser said. He was still holding the stick and looking coldly angry, but he did not once point the stick toward Miskasquamish.

Sometimes, Miskasquamish thought as he walked away, I wish I had never become a man of medicine. The stick of metal was serious magic, but the story about the Builders who fought each other was even more worrying. Obviously, there were no real men of medicine among the white people. Their men of medicine had *all* become Reversers.

"An eye for an eye," Colonel Muadhen kept saying. "An eye for an eye. An eye for an eye."

Lieutenant Brian O'Mara had assumed command and ordered Seamus tied to his horse, like a wounded

man, because O'Mara didn't know what else to do
with a colonel in that condition.

"Can the doctors help in a case like this?" asked
Sergeant Liam de Burke, riding up alongside the lieutenant.

"That I do not know," Lieutenant O'Mara said quietly. "I think only time heals this kind of wound,
faith."

"An eye for an eye," Seamus repeated, not seeing
them. "An eye for an eye. The Lord is a man of war.
The Lord is his name."

"Jesus," de Burke said. "Two years I've served under him. Never did I think Colonel Muadhen would
come to this."

"An eye for an eye," Seamus said, looking at them
intently but vacantly. *"Their infants shall be dashed
into pieces.* Hosea 13, verse 16. *The Lord is a man of
war.* Exodus 15, verse 3. An eye for an eye. The separate and equal Station to which the laws of Nature
and Nature's God entitle them. Our great big murder
and torture machine made by our loving Father in
Heaven."

One day Lady Maria Babcock discovered that Paddy
the Dog had almost died but had recovered very
quickly and unexpectedly.

Paddy the Dog was a huge, friendly, bright-eyed
Irish wolfhound, about twelve years old, with the unthinking natural dignity that was only to be found in
large dogs or Anglican bishops. When Paddy's previous owner died, John had taken custody of the poor
old bright-eyed hound, not wishing to see the misfortunate animal put down. The dog had been called
Paddy then, but, with the influx of Irish farm workers
in the Lousewartshire region, there were dozens and

scores of Paddies around and everybody had developed the habit of calling the Babcock hound, Paddy the Dog.

The day after Paddy the Dog became ill and suddenly recovered—he seemed to have had some sort of heart attack—Maria observed that Cook was extremely agitated whenever Ursula came past the kitchen garden with the huge Irish hound, who even on all fours was a head higher than her. Paddy the Dog had always been tolerant of the children and usually friendly with them in a considerate but haughty way, but he was a "one-man dog" and his special bond had always been with John. Now the animal seemed to have switched his hulking ungainly love to Ursula.

At teatime, Maria invited Ursula to join her in the Rose Room, instead of taking tea (as usual) with her governess, Miss Chaney.

"I have been informed that Paddy the Dog was unwell yesterday," Maria said after they had discussed Ursula's lessons for a while.

The little girl looked up with a grin. You couldn't call it a smile; that much self-satisfaction combined with that much innocence were only possible in the very young, and together they made for an impudent grin. "*I* made him better," Ursula said, as free of guile as Paddy the Dog himself. Her hair was black as Maria's but her complexion showed John's Anglo-Norman ancestry. *Bright as a penny, that one,* Kyte often said.

"And where, pray, did you learn to be a veterinarian?" Maria asked severely.

"Oh, M*ama!*" Ursula was too mature, at seven, to be oblivious to irony. "I am not a vete'nerian, Mama. I just did what you do when the roses are turning poorly."

"Ve*terin*arian," Maria corrected automatically. She had not been aware that Ursula had observed her use of Craft horticulture. But this little "natural philosopher," as John called her, didn't miss much; she was always trying to deduce how things *worked*.

"Vetreremarian," Ursula corrected herself hopefully.

"Veterinarian, darling."

"Veterinarian."

"Very good! Now just one more time."

"Vetrerimarian."

"No. You had it right a second ago, dear.

"Vet-er-in-arian."

"Excellent. Do you wish some more jam?"

"Yes, Mama."

Maria spread the jam on a scone and then asked casually, "What did you do for Paddy the Dog exactly?"

"I told you, Mama. What you do for the roses and other flowers. I held my hands over him and closed my eyes to concentrate."

"In what condition was the poor animal?"

"Like the mare who had to be put down last winter. He couldn't walk or do hardly anything. He just lay there, with his eyes all full of pain. It made me cry, Mama, he looked so pitiful."

"And what happened when you concentrated?" Maria was very glad they were alone in the tearoom.

"Oh, that was grand, Mama. My hands got all warm and I could feel a wonderful light, all golden, coming out of them."

"And then Paddy the Dog was up and running around and having a splendid time," Maria said simply. "Is that not right, darling?"

"Yes, Mama. Am I not a quick learner?"

"Bright as a penny," Maria said, quoting Kyte. "To whom have you spoken about this?"

Ursula frowned, trying to remember. "To Miss Chaney," she said finally.

"Only to her?"

"Oh, yes, and Cook. She asked me if Paddy the Dog was better and I told her I made him better 'cause I felt sorry for him."

Maria spread some more jam on her own biscuit, thinking. Cook was superstitious, but ferociously loyal to the Babcocks. No problem there. And Miss Chaney, thank heavens, was a dogmatic Rationalist. She would attribute the child's story to "imagination." Even if she had seen the healing, she would call it "coincidence." Sometimes, Maria thought, a closed mind can be Our greatest ally, when it denies that We are here.

"Darling," Maria said carefully, "do you know what a secret is?"

"Oh, yes, Mama!" Ursula was thrilled. "The Greystoke twins, they have a secret society for girls. No boys or grownups allowed. And they taught me their password, but I mayn't tell it to you, because you are grown up. I shall tell you when you grow down again."

Ursula had said things like that before, but Maria understood for the first time that the little philosopher had deduced by some logic of symmetry that, just as children eventually grow up, adults correspondingly grow down. Now was not the time to try to correct that clever, if incorrect, biological theory.

"Well," Maria said, "now you and I are going to form a secret society of our own. It is called, ah, the Greensleeve Girls. And the first rule is that we must never, never brag or boast about anything and we never never talk about the healings we do . . ."

"Oh, Mama," Ursula said excitedly, "what shall be our password?"

"Hosea," Seamus said, looking at the hospital ceiling but seeing nothing. "The infants shall be smashed in the day of my wrath. Heh heh. Deuteronomy. I will cover the land with blood. Nature and Nature's God are a fine pair of bloody maniacs. Heh heh heh."

The doctor ordered more laudanum.

Miskasquamish dreamed that the bear-people had gone to the star-people to complain about him and the star-people agreed that he had done bad magic, so they gave the bear-people permission to kill him and eat him.

That was a serious dream, he knew, and it was more serious when, in the morning, he found fresh bear tracks all around his tipi. I shall soon be quite dead at last in spite of all.

Diversion, perversion, subversion, diversion: four giants at four corners.

He erased the tracks quickly, so the tribe would not see them and be frightened. He smoked the healing herb and thought long and hard that morning. It was as he had expected: The Reverser was beginning to reverse all laws. *"Our Lady has gone crazy."*

That afternoon he dressed as a woman and went to the Reverser again. He brought more furs than they had exchanged since the beginning. He also brought his most powerful herbs but did not see any pressing need to mention that fact aloud.

"Mishashamack," the Reverser said cordially, making the peace sign with his arm. He pretended not to notice that the old man was dressed as a squaw.

"Sigamoondo."

The Reverser took the furs with exclamations of pleasure, and then he produced more sparkling red and green crystals from his beltbag. "These are most wonderful furs," he said, "and you are a most generous man."

Miskasquamish took the jewels. "These are crystals beautiful beyond all speech and you are more generous than me."

They sat and Miskasquamish filled the pipe, including the three herbs of truth. He lit it carefully and politely passed it over, knowing the full terror of the risk he was running, but determined to go ahead. Diversion, perversion, subversion, diversion. An eye for an eye.

Sigismundo toked deeply on the pipe, pretending he was not aware of what was happening but wondering what new herbs Miskasquamish was trying this time. Then he handed the pipe back and passed through a period of glaciations and altercations with emerald troglodytes to arrive at a seemingly endless series of tipis, wigwams, igloos, yurts, pagodas, pyramids, haciendas, geodesic domes, mosques, Greek temples, Gothic cathedrals, termite hills, beaver dams, treks across nameless deserts to forbidden cities, moving slowly past the eyeless eaters, the crab-people, the dholes and shoggoths, the chocolate mouse, the giant rabbit, the frammisgoshes, the wan love-worn fur, the horse of another color, the peppermint sine waves and finding it altogether a novel experience and singularly fnord farble of his kind of inward-turning spiral effect.

"Thank you," he said politely, wondering what the next few minutes would be like.

* * *

The doctor asked Seamus, kindly, if he knew where he was.

"I am in a army field hospital," Seamus said. "In the colony of New York. I am not mad, sir. I am only extremely nervous. Extremely high strung, you might say. The Lord is a man of war, you know. An eye for an eye."

"Do you know how many days you've been here?"

"No." Seamus was surprised at that. "I am only nervous now, but perhaps I was not fully in possession of all my faculties for a time. I have seen war and hell, Doctor, and they are much the same."

"Do you remember how you got here?"

"An eye for an eye," Seamus said. "Do you know that way of it, Doctor? An eye for an eye, we say. An eye for an eye—it's our whole law and religion. The Lord is a man of war. Exodus. And that way we go, an eye for an eye and an eye for an eye and we all end up fooken blind."

The doctor told the staff to keep Colonel Muadhen on laudanum for a few more days. The prognosis seemed good, and he expected a full recovery. "What the hell did the poor man see in Cherry Valley?" he asked a subaltern.

"I don't know, sir. And frankly I don't want to know."

"War," the doctor said. "Christ, I'll be glad when it's over."

"They killed your father," Miskasquamish said.

"Yes." I am in my mother's room.

"It was a terrible death. I see him. He looks like one other man I saw tortured that terribly, a man who had offended the Iroquois people. There are good people and bad people and very bad people and then there are those damned Iroquois.''

"My father had fallen into the hands of Neapolitans. They are somewhat like the Iroquois of the Mediterranean.''

"You hated him.''

"Yes.'' He had a horse named a procession of the damned.

"But you hated the way he died..''

Children, Seamus said. *Little children. Infants, some of them. They sounded like cats howling. Like cats screeching as their tails were pulled off them.*

The Lord is a man of war: the Lord is His name.

Sigismundo began to cry, not like a man but like a boy. He cried for a long time. Miskasquamish waited.

Sigismundo pushed open the door of M.M.M. "Mystical Books of All Ages'' and passed through the Parthenon, St. Peter's, grim Gothic banks, universities, nunneries, Irish castles, chemical laboratories, botanical gardens, one nude one cat, gingerbread houses, the order of arachnids, bakeries, sea lampreys, the order of chondrichthyes, the Father of Waters, the Centipede Police, one nut one squatter, the order of Memphis and Mizraim. And the ants came marching one by one. The million colors of the rainbow appeared in the dew drop on a single blade of grass. And the ants came marching two by two. Sir John Babcock walked out of the log cabin carrying the stone Sigismundo had himself carried in his fourth degree Mark Master initiation, with the words *Et in Arcadia ego.* And the ants came marching three by three. He was in a ship that sailed under the water instead of on top of the water. And the ants came marching four by four.

Peppino chanted, ''Mother Tana, who is the green earth! Mother Tana, who is our red rage! Mother Tana, who is also called Isis and Magdalene!'' You see it looking at you, kid. Four giants at four corners. Matter, markery, look-see, and wan.

Sigismundo retched and clutched the tree as the world spun. A procession of the damned. Hamnet, Shakespeare's son, had a mongoose. Complicated gears and levers escaped from a definition: The quick claw snatched a canape.

Miskasquamish waited. Keen. Able. Coyne. Abel.

"The son of my father's brother," Sigismundo said. "He had the Evil Talk sickness. He jumped into the water."

"Yes. You have told me. I see him."

"He thought the woman-men were persecuting him. He thought they were everywhere."

"Yes. In the Evil Talk sickness you attack the world, while thinking it is attacking you."

"It is the sickness you have," Sigismundo said abruptly.

"No. You talk foolishly now."

"It is the same sickness with you," Sigismundo repeated, panting. "With Antonio, the enemy was the women-men. With you, it is the bear-people. It is the same sickness." It was as hopeless as arguing with Peppino. All the men of medicine were sick. Humanity was sick. The universe itself was sick. And I, Sigismundo thought, may be sickest of all right now.

"No. The bear-people hate me for magic I did against them once."

"It is you who hates yourself. The bear-people do not remember your magic. I am not a Reverser. There are no Reversers. You invented the Reversers to explain things you could not understand. It is in your head." Sigismundo was panting more desperately, to get some air in him, as if he had the heart-bursting disease. "Antonio and the women-men, you and the bear-people, me and my damned murdering father. It is all the same sickness. The world is sick and we try to cure one another."

Then he would not sit upright any longer and sprawled on the ground, still panting, but not able to weep any longer. Brodarmord: one thousand and ten and four. The ants came marching four by four.

The bear-people were walking all over the clearing, grunting and muttering curses against Miskasquamish and the Maheema tribe. Miskasquamish avoided looking directly at them. Diversion, perversion, subversion, diversion.

"There is one mind inside all things," Sigismundo said. "The Wakan." He meant to say: There are no bear-people, only the Wakan.

"No. The Wakan is not a mind. If it were a mind, it would make sense. The Wakan contains all things, is all things, so it does not need to make sense. You want it to make sense and that is why you became a Reverser." He meant: The bear-people and the Maheema people must be at war. The Wakan is not *One*, but all. It includes opposites.

Sigismundo thought, *How do I know what he meant?* But he said, "There are no real bears here."

When laws are outlawed, only outlaws will have laws.

"None." The old man was afraid, but still brave and stubborn. Thunderclouds and ball lightning useful to the nation. Separate and equal Stations. Procrastination. Fulmination.

"But you see bears and are afraid," Sigismundo said, panting on the ground. "I can tell that much about you after all these moons."

Miskasquamish could not deny it with the truth

herbs in him. "Now we must go in the yellow brook
and sweat," he said. That was the best way, with the
truth herbs.

"I cannot walk."

"You will crawl then."

Miskasquamish walked past the bear-people. They
growled and made angry faces but his magic kept them
from becoming completely solid and they could not
hurt him. He came to the hot yellow brook and removed his women's clothes. He lowered himself into
the water, hot against his naked body, and sweated.
He began merging with the water, the earth, the trees,
the clouds. Being a man of medicine was a funny joke,
he remembered. Sometimes it took the truth herbs to
remember things like that. The Maheema tribe were a
funny joke, too. All people were funny jokes: Each
tribe was a different kind of joke. Even the bear-people
and the Reverser were funny jokes. He laughed and
sweated his way through.

Sigismundo was crawling around the earth above
him. "Get damned shirt off," he was saying. "Can't
get damned shirt off." Then he was naked and slid
slippery down the bank of mud into the hot yellow
brook. "What was that stuff we smoked?" he asked.
The Indian did not reply—he was off on the other side
of the moon, it seemed. "Just want to live in the woods
and have some peace," Sigismundo complained.
"Another God-damned magician comes along to take
me on another God-damned guided tour of Chapel
Perilous. The Rosy Cross is everywhere. Oh, well,"
he said philosophically, "death by water. That was the
prophecy."

They sweated their way through this part of it in the
hot sulphur water. Coyne. Abel. Cain. Apple. Fire
and water are one. Brotharmurd, a law.

"Antonio jumped because he imagined the sod-
omists were combining against him," Sigismundo explained patiently. "You are imagining that the bears
are combining against you. It is all imagination. *I* do
not need to be cured. *You* need to be cured."

The Indian sweated, eyes closed, riding through it.

There was no hope for him this time: It was the third
stroke. Sulphur and damnation and one imbecile.

The whole of nature was identified as a mongoose.

"Very well," Sigismundo said, willing to compro-
mise. "We both need to be cured."

The earth stopped moving. They entered eternity
together.

On Midwinter Night, Maria and her "women's study
group" were doing healings for friends when the cone
of power suddenly arose and Maria became totally one
with Greensleeves. "The future will differ very greatly
from the past," she said dramatically.

That did not disturb anybody: Greensleeves often
said things like that, obvious platitudes until you
thought of them again a few weeks later and realized
they had more than one meaning.

Maria danced around the circle, kissing the other
twelve women. She kissed them erotically, sensually,
then burst away, laughing, and boldly removed her
clothes to stand naked in ecstasy. "To me, to me,"
she cried and then she danced wildly.

That was not too unusual, either. The women all
knew that Greensleeves was somewhat free and libertine at times.

Then Maria scared hell out of them.

"The poor infants," she screamed. "In the snow."
She started to weep hysterically. "My God, what are
they doing to the infants?" Maria howled shrilly, with

the horror of a new Canto for Dante's *Inferno* in her voice. The group waited for Kyte to direct them, but the old lady just watched Maria intently, until the weeping was replaced by anger as quickly as it had just replaced sexuality.

"Cruel, terrible men," Maria shouted. "We must go to the War Office in London and make them stop this vile war. I will lead you. They will listen to me."

That was the way to get yourself lodged in "Bedlam"—St. Mary's of Bethlehem Hospital for the insane, in London. Everybody looked at Kyte, hoping she would act now. Kyte was the one who knew what to do when Greensleeves became too much like a goddess of love and lost all human rationality.

"Join hands," Kyte said simply. "She ain't in no real danger as yet. We shall guide her, have no fear. It is a mere passin' of the Abyss."

None of the other women had seen a "passin' of the Abyss" before, but Kyte was the oldest and most experienced, and seemed to know what she was doing. None of them guessed she was as frightened as any of them, so they joined hands and sang as Kyte guided them.

> *Who is she that sang so fair*
> *Shed such treasure in the air?*
> *Who is she*
> *O who is she*
> *That laughed among the flowers*
> *For two eternal hours?*
> *Who is she*
> *O who is she*
> *With skirt of moss and hair of leaves?*
> *Who but our Lady Greensleeves?*

* * *

"Novus ordo seclorem," Maria began chanting. "Our Lady has gone crazy. *Novus ordo seclorem.* Our Lady has gone crazy." Keen. Able. Coyne. Abel. Cain. Apple.

A tall red-headed man climbed out of the yellow water shouting, "You will, by God, obey my orders, sir, or I will eat your liver, sir! Do you hear me? You feeble-minded, block-headed, whiskey-soaked son of a ring-tailed hog by a purple-pricked chimpanzee!! *Do you hear me, sir?"*

He has a horse named Copenhagen, would you believe it?

To Maria, now, it seemed that Greensleeves, the female body of the planet, was not only crazy but had also turned into a man. A man with a bronze skin, naked, in a yellow bubbling brook.

"It is the class of all minds," Sigismundo said thoughtfully.

"Our lady has gone crazy. Why else would she let the poor infants be mutilated in that foul way? An eye for an eye."

We don't got to show you no steeenking reality.

A procession of the damned in my mother's room. The whole of nature was identified as a horse named Copenhagen, would you believe it? Hamnet, Shakespeare's son, died at the age of eleven years. He had a mongoose named four hundred imbeciles to spring your trap. But the caves below Napoli were still dark and haunted by goat-headed men, and Peppino still held out the Devil's Book and pricked Sigismundo's thumb for blood, and guided his hand and he signed his soul away forever.

When marriage is outlawed, only outlaws will have in-laws.

"Hell of a medicine man," Sigismundo complained weakly, exhausted. "Won't talk to me at the crucial point. Leaves me to talk to myself. Very well, then. All I've been through hasn't been enough. There's more to come. Peppino never left me. I still have to fight one more battle with him. Oedipus wrecks."

Nature's God, the bronze naked man, was sweating, eyes closed, letting the magic work without him. Maria moved closer, wanting his Willy inside her, forgetting John, forgetting Christian civilization, alone with Nature and Nature's God.

Male, female, male, female. Coon. Babel. Four giant angels at the four corners in blue, red, yellow, and green. You merely have to wait longer to spring your trap.

"The first time I saw you, in a dream, was twelve years ago," Sigismundo said. "Year I met my father, too. I was fourteen years old then. 1764. You and my father and Frankenstein, all in one year. Hell of a lot to deal with, when you're fourteen. Matter of fact, you look a bit like Frankenstein, with a heavy tan. Or is that the herbs? Maybe everybody looks like Frankenstein. Can't tell. Only two of us here."

The bears circled the brook, grunting, growling. Next we will hear of a pig with wings.

"Go away," Sigismundo said. "You're supposed to be in his head, not mine. He has a simple mind, really. He does magic against you, so you do magic against him. Then he does more magic against you and you do more magic against him. An eye for an eye. Round and round on the circle that never ends. He thinks it balances out, because the Wakan is on both sides all the time. If he were civilized, he'd decide you were 'evil' and set out to exterminate you. That's progress, according to the wisest men of our age."

Sigismundo suddenly saw roads running through the woods, and the roads had no cobblestones but were smooth like an English lawn, and people rode on them without horses, in his autokinotons. And the people were all Scotch-Irish Americans with accents mixed of New York and Baltimore elements but when they stopped their autokinotons and went into the underwater log cabin (which he called a tipi because Mishashamck did not know the word "cabin") it was now a Pizza Ristorante and had scampi and other Neapolitan dishes. And a sign said "DAYTON 20 MILES."

"I call it a mind," he said, "because it is more like a mind than anything else, but it is not really a mind."

"It is a human mind in a human head," Miskasquamish said suddenly. "In a raccoon, it is a racoon. In a rock, it is a rock. It is not a mind because it does not have to make sense. It only has to survive, which is easy because it never dies, only changes. The Wakan. I call it that because nobody knows its real name."

Apple. Coin. Hobble. Cain. Perversion, diversion, excursion, perversion.

"It is the class of all minds," Sigismundo said thoughtfully, "which is not a mind for the same reason that the class of all Neapolitan violinists is not a Neapolitan violinist. Or the class of all circles is not a circle. Is that it?"

Dr. Cyprus rose from the well and said distinctly. "The path up is the path down. The way forward is the way back. The universe inside is outside but the universe outside is inside. I am most useful to government officials." He donned a Siberian fur coat, held his nose, and dived back into the well. His hand arose from the water, holding aloft a sword with a handle like flame and on it the initials. S.B.

Maria began weeping again over the tiny infant bodies in the red snow. To Miskasquamish this was the crucial point of the journey of the three truth herbs: seeing the mother of the bear-people, the oldest goddess of the tribe, weeping in pain. This was what his magic had done to her and her people. He had only intended to protect the Maheema tribe, not to cause so much suffering to the bear-people.

He held up his arm in the peace sign to her. He climbed from the brook, naked, and stood unarmed before her. He would accept the judgment, whatever it was. He knew his guilt. "An eye for an eye and we all go blind," he said.

"Help the poor children dying in the snow," she cried, weeping.

> Who is she
> Say, who is she
> With eye so bold and smile so free?
> Great Mother of God
> Say, who is she
> To bring such bliss
> With every kiss
> And medicine each heart that grieves?
> Who but my lady Greensleeves?

Paddy the Dog raised his head in a long mournful howl like a banshee. "It is the black curse of the O'Tooles," Seamus said.

Sigismundo looked into Maria's eyes and knew she was mad with what Miskasquamish would normally call the Evil Talk sickness, but Miskasquamish now seemed to think she was Artemis or the local equiva-

lent of Artemis—some bear goddess or bare goddess—
and, at the same time, Sigismundo thought, *Now at
last we are naked together* as if all the fantasies of his
adolescence were coming true.

"Here I am again," he said aloud. "Two lunatics
for company and not entirely sure of my own sanity.
Actaeon. Artemis and Hermes. Tom, Dick, and Harry.
Shem, Ham, and Japhet, the Three Ruffians. The Holy
Trinity. I am who Am: *Et in Arcedia ego.* Or some-
thing."

Miskasquamish was no longer Frankenstein; now he
was old Abraham Orfali. Fellow of the Rose Cross.
Sigismundo's first teacher in the Cabala.

Abraham handed Sigismundo a ritual dagger.
"Death by water," he said with ritual solemnity. "The
prophecy was ambiguous, but now it must be ful-
filled."

"You mean I must—"

"Yes," the old Cabalist said. "It is the only way to
save her. You must make the supreme magical sacrifice. Your very heart."

Every initiation in every degree of Freemasonry had
some symbolic echo of the Crucifixion in it. Sigismundo suddenly understood that eventually the symbolism becomes reality. You don't become one with
Christ until you are nailed to the Rose Cross.

Sigismundo looked again at Maria's naked beauty.
He knew that he simply wanted to take her sexually. He
was not Jesus and he was not even Don Quixote. He did
not want to die for her. The romantic love of his adolescence had been mere lust all the time, just as his hatred
of Peppino was a desire to be as cruel as Peppino.
Why deceive himself further and pretend grandiose
things? He was no Redeemer, and not even a hero of
a novel—just a musician who wanted to be left alone

to write music. *"Now at last I am free of the damnable books of Romance."*

"Now," Abraham said. "No more hesitation. In a few more moments it will be too late, and she will be mad as Antonio forever."

Sigismundo raised the dagger to his breast. I've done many brave things, he thought unemotionally, because I was ashamed to have people think me a coward. Will I keep up the mask to the ultimate, and kill myself rather than admit everything I do is motivated by selfishness and the wish to be admired? His hand trembled. There was more than lust in his feeling for Maria now; if his feeling was not romantic love out of a book, then perhaps it was human compassion. She was in terrible danger, and he alone could save her. That was the logic of things, out here beyond space and time and matter, in the heart of creation.

The bear-people were changing. Some were Chinese and some were Hindus and some were Arabs and some were Europeans and many were men of medicine from nearby tribes or from tribes far away in Africa. They were all helping at this crucial moment. Sigismundo saw rows and rows of flying bombs—the bombs that would exist when his autokinoton had wings and flew across the sky, and then lost the wings to fly faster. The autokinoton of the future would go to the moon and back, but the crazy men would rather use it for bombs. And all the flying bombs would be set off at once and life on earth would die, unless history changed.

"The poor children in the snow," Maria cried.

Sigismundo cut his chest. Blood flowed. It was a hesitation scratch, no more. He understood that his cowardice was stronger than desire to be good or seem good to others and even stronger than his pity for the mad woman he once thought he loved.

"To save Maria," Abraham said. "To save the world from the bombs that fly."

"No," Sigismundo cried. "No. No. No. No. I *am* a Reverser, God damn it. I don't have to be the bloody hero of the story all the time. I might make a hell of a good villain if I set my mind to it. I have had enough of magic and initiations. Now, I want to live. *My* way. *Tenebo, illegitimati: perdurabo!*"

"There is always one more initiation," Abraham said.

"HA!" It was the voice of Peppino Balsamo, Sigismundo's true father. "You are my son, remember. You signed your name in the Devil's book when I commanded. At last you are coming to your senses. I was your true teacher all the time. To hell with this Christian sentimentality, boy. Better the whole world should burn to cinder and blow away than a free man should deny his desires. Take the bitch and fuck her."

The future will differ very greatly from the past.

In whom do you set your faith? Abraham had asked six years ago.

In my Self, Sigismundo replied.

A magical vow cannot be broken. You think it can, but it cannot.

Sigismundo turned to Abraham. "Build a grave," he said quickly. "Write on it, *Sigismundo Balsamo.* Not *Celine* or *Malatesta,* God damn it. *Balsamo.* And write under it, *The Father lives in the Son.*" To Peppino, he added, with acceptance of all the opposites, "Father, it is finished."

Then he cut out his heart with one quick red slash across the breast and dropped dead at Maria's feet, falling inward and downward through the endless spiral.

Maria Babcock knelt, white-faced, and touched the bloody heart still pulsating on the ground. As her fingers touched the moist organ, it became only an autumn leaf. A dead yellow leaf, blowing in the wind. She looked around slowly. Old Kyte and the others in the coven were watching her.

"You do not know the goddess," Maria said simply, "until you suffer with her, for all her sons and daughters." Her eyes were sane again.

And Old Kyte smiled serenely, for Maria had crossed the Abyss, and now Kyte knew for sure who would succeed her as High Priestess.

Sigismundo Balsamo sat meditating.

He had learned in Egypt that meditation, when near to clear Mind, was apt to be interrupted by explosive eruptions from the dream-soul. He knew the psychological basis of St. Anthony being assaulted by demons in the desert, Buddha being attacked by the Lord of Hallucinations before Awakening, Parcifal's excursion into the Chapel Perilous before finding the Grail. That was the logic of the Widow's Son: You could only rise as high above ordinary mind as you were able to sink below it.

He had all along regarded the crazy shaman Miskasquamish as a part of himself, a portion of his own mind that needed purification.

Now his meditation had been shaken rather roughly by the latest encounter with Miskasquamish and the herbs of truth. Maria and Abraham Orfali and Peppino and all the figures he loved and hated before his Awakening in Egypt had been involved this time, and he was still attached to them by his emotions. Obviously, most of what he had seen was hallucination. Or was it the final initiation? Whatever it was that happened to him siting under that tree, he had made a real choice. He had decided he knew what a Reverser was and he did not really want to be one of them. Now he was curious about how much of this had been his mind playing games—all of it, or only parts of it?

Sigismundo shot a turkey to eat that night and then went in search of the local Indians.

He hiked all day and then lit a bonfire. Alone, listening to the nightbirds call, he cleaned and plucked the dead turkey. Alone, under the stars, far from Europe and hermetic societies, he thought of the Indians and their own kind of magic as he ate the turkey. He had come a long, long way from the boy in Napoli who wanted to write great music and stay away from troubles of all sorts. The sky was bigger than ever and there were many orders of intelligence in it.

He arose at sunup and began his trek again. By noon, he found an encampment of the nomadic Maheema. His mastery of their language was not as good as it had seemed when he was having his spirit dialogues with Miskasquamish, but they were friendly and eager to exchange news and gossip. There were many white settlers in Ohio by then, and the Maheema were not surprised by Sigismundo's skin or his odd clothes.

They told him, yes, they had had a medicine man named Miskasquamish once. That was a long time ago, though.

Miskasquamish had been killed by a bear over fifty years ago, in 1730 on Sigismundo's calendar. He had screamed horribly because, with all his courage, he had always been afraid of bears.

10. The Pursuit of Wild Pigs

New York–Virginia 1778–1781

winds like the Wrath of God

The war for American independence dragged on. And on. And on.

Seamus Muadhen had been released from the Army field hospital with no further symptoms—except for a heightened suspicion that Nature's God was not merely indifferent but actively nefarious—and endured all of it.

He was in the midst of the most pitiful and uninspiring army ever to march. As everybody has heard, the soldiers were so ill clothed that their naked feet left bloodstains on the ground in the worst of the winter months, but shoes were only a small part of what they lacked. At the battle of Monmouth, neither coats nor trousers had arrived to replace those worn to useless rags months earlier, and one fourth of the Continental soldiers charged the British guns wearing no more than shirts. Nor had they been better clothed for most of the war.

Faith, Seamus thought often, *I've heard of ragged-arsed armies but we must be the first bare-arsed army in history.*

Congress eventually received the money the ingenious Dr. Franklin and the intransigent Mr. Adams had borrowed in France and Holland, but very little of it was spent of the welfare of the troops. The little that was actually allotted for the soldiers mostly went to profiteers and the Army remained hungry and nearly naked.

General Washington raged and ranted, and informed Congress that the food that did occasionally come through to his troops was "unfit for horses and cattle." Various government officials wrote him apologetic letters and assured him that they were working on the problem. Food remained scarce and unpalatable.

Washington had a cunning strategy, or a fantasy dreamed up while smoking those heathen Indian herbs—Seamus was never sure which—that involved forced marches of twenty-four or even forty-eight hours without pause or rest. This allowed the Continental Army to seemingly disappear like a conjurer's rabbit from the territory where the British expected to find them and then reappear, shockingly, howling like demons on the attack, where the British thought they could not possibly be. It was the best possible strategy under the circumstances—and was later emulated by other revolutionary guerrilla armies—but Seamus sometimes thought it would eventually kill more of the troops than the whole British Army and their Hessian and Indian allies could kill.

In the winters, dressed in rags or less, sometimes unfed for weeks on end, the soldiers on a forced march of forty-eight hours would look and act like the walking dead. One private, a Joseph Plumb Martin of Massachusetts, later wrote, "I have felt more anxiety, undergone more fatigue and hardships, suffered more in every way, in performing one of these tedious marches than ever I did in fighting the hottest battle I was ever engaged in.'' Colonel Muadhen was forever anxious that his troops would crack entirely and march on after finally ordered to stop—stumbling and weaving in a drunken-looking shambles till they fell miles away, like horses with the blind staggers.

The food continually promised to the troops arrived weeks late in the best cases and often never arrived at all. ''Sure, we had bugger all to eat last week,'' Lieutenant O'Mara said once, ''and I expect less than that this week.'' Seamus copied the procedure of other officers and allowed his men to hunt whenever Washington did not have them on another forced march. The most plentiful game to be found was wild pig, and the happiest days were those on which two or more pigs were shot. Everybody would gather around the campfires where the pigs were roasted; some men were so desperately hungry they would burn their fingers reaching in to get a bite before the pig was fully cooked.

We started out seeking what Mr. Jefferson called life, liberty, and the pursuit of happiness, Seamus thought. Now we are fighting on, stubbornly and almost insanely, for life, liberty and the pursuit of wild pigs. Were Mr. Jefferson's words some evil sorcery that drove men mad and led them to destroy themselves attempting the impossible? Was he, like General Washington, another bloody Freemason and involved in heathen magic of some sort?

But Seamus became an excellent pig hunter himself, and he was happier and felt more triumphant after killing one pig than after killing twenty Redcoats. Unlike the British, the pigs did not have guns and couldn't shoot back, and it was not against law or nature to eat them when they were dead. Besides, they existed everywhere the Continental Army roamed, God's plenty of them, and the beef continually promised by the War Office existed evidently only as a word on paper—or when it did arrive it was like a fairy's dinner, as Lieutenant O'Mara said, having devil a bit in the way of fat and even less nor that in the way of lean.

I know why *I* go on fighting, Seamus thought one night, during another interminable forced march. I'm simply mad, and that's the whole of it. I went off my head when Corporal Murphy was torturing me back in Dun Laoghaire, or when my soul left my body at the battle of Brandywine, or when I saw those poor little mutilated babies in Cherry Valley. I have bees in my bonnet or bats in my belfy or owls in my attic or some such Irish affliction. But why do these other poor buggers struggle on? Had Jefferson and his friend Tom Paine indeed put a spell on them?

He looked at the men marching, half-naked, a seemingly endless troop of hollow-eyed skeletal figures, looking for all the world as if some incompetent disciple of Rabbi Low of Prague had created a regiment of Golems and forgot to include brains or a sense of direction before turning them loose. Like the alleged *zombis* of the Caribbean. Like damned souls circling their cells in Dante's inferno. Why did they go on?

Seamus understood what it meant to hate the British and to long for freedom from British domination; to be Irish was to be born with such knowledge even before you discovered how to find your mother's nipple and get your gums around it. But even hatred of conquerors and love of liberty must have some limit in a sane world, and that limit had surely been passed long ago. Why did these half-human creatures still stumble on in the dark—sleepless, foodless, mostly garmentless, losing most battles, only succeeding occasionally in hit-and-run attacks that killed a lot of Redcoats but did not really change the balance of power?

War does that to you, Seamus decided. *Sure, they are all as mad as I am by now.*

Sometimes Seamus thought the nights of rest were worse than the nights of marching. New England seemed to have nine months of winter and three months of bad weather, and Pennsylvania was much the same. Even when there was no snow or freezing cold—even in what passed for summer—it seemed to rain uncommonly often, and blankets were another item the Congress had forgotten to send in adequate supply. Most of the men slept on the ground covered only by the same ragged and filthy clothing in which they marched and fought—clothing with as many holes as the moon has craters. At best, in the rains, they woke half buried in puddles of cold rain and slippery mud. But at worst—which seemed more normal—the freezing snows would cover them as they slept and some would never wake at all.

There was occasional relief. One week in '79—or was in '80? Seamus was never sure after—his platoon was actually given a fine old mansion to live in. The owners, he was told, were Tories who had fled on the approach of the Continentals. The officers slept in beds; the men on floors—but without rain or snow falling on them, it seemed like paradise.

One slave had remained in the house, an old toothless woman. She claimed not to know what had happened to the other slaves: Seamus guessed that, as on other occasions of this sort, they had simply taken to the woods and were surviving, much like the Army, by hunting wild pigs and trying to learn to sleep in rain and snow without dying of it. The old woman also declared her undying loyalty to "good king George" and roundly asserted that the Rebels would all be hanged eventually and then burn in hell for eternity.

"Thank you kindly for your counsel," Seamus said to her after her diatribe. "It is like sweet music to hear a female voice again."

The men ate every edible crop and all the animals on the land and stole all the clothes in the house. Seamus hadn't seen so many happy faces since the damned interminable war started: They had ducks one day and geese another and glutted on pork and beef and feasted on turkey, and most of the men got coats and shoes again; it was a glorious week altogether. The old Black woman cursed them continually and warned them, in colorful details, what God thought of Rebels and thieves. Then the order came to move on—another forced march had been decreed.

The old Black woman cursed them one more time as they left. Poor thing, Seamus thought, she expects her Master back tomorrow and has no conception of how long this bloody war is probably going to last; and what will she do when Master doesn't return? Seamus had learned enough of American ways to know that "house niggers" had no knowledge of field work—the old woman could serve the proper food on the proper plates, but would have no idea how the food found its way into the kitchen before she started to prepare it. It might have been deposited by fairies for all she knew to the contrary. She was alone and helpless, unless the "field niggers" found life in the wilderness so appalling that they decided to return.

He soon forgot the old woman. There were more forced marches, more battles, more gnawing hunger.

One day a sergeant from the quartermaster corps

drove up in a wagon full of hogsheads of whiskey. The
men, malnourished as they were, raised a commotion
of complaint when they discovered there was no food
aboard the wagon—proof at last, Seamus thought, that
there are cases when even an Irishman would rather
eat than booze—but when their hogshead was un-
loaded, they became reconciled.

"Whiskey is better nor bugger all," Lieutenant
O'Mara said cheerfully and the hogshead was opened
and the gargle began to flow.

There were no sounds for a while except long loud
liquid gurgles and long low contented sighs and occasional cries of, "Here now, mate, pass it on." For
once it wasn't raining or snowing and everybody's
mood began to improve.

"Well," O'Mara said, "if the Congress thinks we
can win a war on whiskey instead of solid food, by
Christ maybe we can."

Somebody else began to sing softly:

> In Scarlet Town where I was born
> There was a fair maid dwellin'
> Made all the lads cry 'Well-a-day!'
> And her name was Barbara Allen

Other voices joined in and the ballad of hard-hearted
Barbara proceeded melodiously, except for occasional
cries of, "You bastard, pass it on now. The rest of us
have a thirst, too."

Two hours later, the whiskey—intended to be a
week's supply—was gone, and suddenly the order came
down: Another forced march was beginning.

Oh, bejesus, Seamus thought. *If I'm to navigate*

these drunken sods through the wilderness in the dark, it will be a greater miracle than anything they tell in the Bible.

The march began, with Seamus's troops weaving about like the Sidewinder, the fabulous snake of the West that the Yankees had told Seamus about. Having paid their respects to Barbara Allen, the men were now inclined to serenade Molly Malone:

> In Dublin's fair city
> Where the girls are so pretty . . .

The song did not last long. There was a fence in the way and the men, full of whiskey and empty of food, began trying to climb over it. Some landed on one side, some on the other, but all were head down and arse upward. "Look at the stars, the stars!" an inebriated voice cried from the heap. "Sure, they are spinning around like children's tops!"

Seamus, wobbling from one side of his horse to the other, rode up to the scene of the pileup and began threatening to shoot if the drunken fools did not get on their feet and start marching again. He was rather proud of his performance at that moment: He was the very image of military Authority, he thought.

Then he fell off his horse. He landed in some lovely mud. It was the most lovely, the most comfortable, the most appealing mud he had ever seen. He decided to take a short nap before considering how to engineer proper military respect amid this eristic chaos of alcoholism. He dozed off planning what he would say when he was strong enough to stand and give orders again. The last thing he heard was a voice trying to start a round of Molly Malone again:

Through streets wide and narrow
She wheeled her wheelbarrow . . .
Crying "Cockles, fresh mussels, alive, alive, oh."

He dreamed he was back in Dublin wandering the
endless labyrinth of crooked and winding old streets
and Molly Malone was serving turkey and ham from
her wheelbarrow, but he could never catch up with
her: She was always around the next turn. Then he was
walking along the quays on the river Anna Liffey and
the British were shelling the town from a gunboat and
General Washington was leading the Rebels in retreat
again and O'Lachlann of Meath, weaving a strange
new flag with a plough and stars on it, said, "War,
one war after another, blood and horror until the end
of time."

When he woke it was morning, and praise God, it
had not rained while they slept. The only consequence
was that everybody had a hangover. Since every platoon had received its own hogshead, and all were
equally famished of food, the whiskey had knocked
everybody over fairly quickly and Seamus's "Fighting
Irish" were in no more disgrace than the rest of the
Army.

The forced march began again. Bleeding Christ,
leading hungry men on a two-day march was never
easy, but when they all start out with hangovers, and
the officers are hung over, too, it is like a quick trot
through one of the lower and less salubrious bolges of
Satan's kingdom of Hell. Seamus felt, through all
forty-eight hours of it, that there were carpenters
building a house in his skull. They had unusually large
hammers and banged away as if determined to finish

the house in a single day. If anyone wanted to see an Irishman who sincerely hated whiskey, Seamus was your man that day.

Mother Church could learn a lot from General Washington, Seamus thought. This was a Lent with a real fast and real mortifications of the flesh. I swear to God, he told himself, if the quartermasters arrive again with grog and no food I will execute them on the spot.

Of course, he knew he would do no such thing. Even in the worst of the hangover, he still treasured the memory of that wonderful night of drunken happiness, with no rain falling and no Redcoats shooting at him. Maybe Congress did have the right idea of how best to fill the stomachs of men engaged in what looked like the losing side of an endless war.

Winter was coming on again—Christ, it seemed as if it was always winter since the bloody war started— and Congress decreed a day of National Thanksgiving. Seamus assumed that Congress was thankful because the loans from France and Holland allowed them to pay their own salaries. He was never informed about what the troops were supposed to be thankful for. Nonetheless, food arrived for the day, and arrived on time, and it consisted of half a cup of rice and a spoon of vinegar for every soldier.

"Faith," said Lieutenant O'Mara, "it's better than eating my boots, especially since I don't have boots at the moment." Others had less sense of humor and the common troops outdid their previous efforts in cursing the damned ungrateful Congress that demanded all of them and gave rice and vinegar in return.

After the feast, the troops were obliged to attend a religious service. The clergyman—representing one of the innumerable sects of Protestants in this religiously

anarchistic society—had evidently never been near
soldiers before and was visibly shaken by the emaci-
ated bodies, dirty faces, stinking rags, and half-dazed,
half-brutalized expressions of the men he saw before
him. For some reason, the parson choose to preach a
sermon on "do violence to no man, speak the truth to
Authority and do not steal that which is thy neighbor's
property."

Maybe, Seamus thought, it was the only sermon this
ninny knew. Or maybe so many stinking bodies had
made him ill and he didn't know where he was. In any
case, the sermon was not a resounding success with
the troops who, after all, were in the habit of doing
violence to the British army, who never spoke total
truth to Authority because they might get court-
martialed if they did commit that indiscretion, and who
lived, much of the time, by stealing crops and animals
from the farms they passed.

Ah, well, Seamus decided, what can you expect of
a bloody clergyman?

Then they were on the march again, this time headed
for a place called Staten Island, where Washington intended to sail the bay and present a surprise to the
British troops. It did not work out that way at all.
Some damned Loyalist had learned the Rebel plans, it
soon appeared, and the British on Staten Island had
their own surprise prepared in advance.

Battle is a business that might loosen your bowels
even in the best case, Seamus thought, but when a
shell starts flying before you even realize fully that you
have walked into a trap, it is worrisome in the extreme.

Seamus saw more of his troops killed that day than
in any other battle and, in the heat of retreat, it tore
at his heart that the poor lads would not even have a

decent burial but would probably be thrown in a common pit.

Well, he told himself, I always knew any man who fights the Almighty British Empire is a damned fool. Why, why, why do I not just slip away some night, find my way to Canada, and enjoy the comforts of an ordinary house servant again?

Why?

It has something to do with General Washington, Seamus thought. *Every time I talk to him I come away believing what he believes: that a Higher Power is guiding and directing him. And it has something to do with the bewitching rhetoric of Mr. Jefferson and Mr. Paine, I think. And it has something to do with years and years of being clever and cunning and never openly defying the damned Brits, until all your cleverness and cunning began to stink like cowardice in your nostrils. It has something to do with six hundred years of brave men in Ireland who were not clever and cunning and did defy the Brits and ended their days hanging from trees; they were damned fools,* Seamus thought, *but at least they lived and died like men, not like gelded house-pets. It has something to with every Irishman having a belly full of being clever and cunning; it was a bursting need to be bloody unreasonable and play against the odds just for once. It has something to do with the way I have hated them since they tortured me in Dun Laoghaire.*

Mostly, Seamus concluded morosely, *it has to do with Nature's God or the Catholic Church's God or both of them. Somehow the gods have put it into my head that even if I doubt them and scorn them, one of them at least is really there and had decided to use me whether I want to be used or not.*

It must be Nature's God. The Pope's God would never incite men to rebellion and anarchy.

No: Nature's God was totally indifferent to men, as He was to lice and fish and dogs. It might be a God that nobody had named yet, a God perhaps struggling to be born: the God that Seamus had spoken to when he was shot out of his body at Brandywine.

The first months of 1780 were worse than Valley Forge. The snow fell day after day. Snow-blindness and the extra problems of marching when giant snow banks hide the men ahead of you added to the misery. Hunger was more extreme than ever. One man acted out Sergeant O'Mara's grim joke and actually did eat one of his boots. In a nearby company, the men conspired to shoot an officer's pet dog and ate it. One week Seamus ate the bark off a tree branch one day and bugger all for the next six days in a row, because the bark kept him nauseous and dizzy for that long.

He maintained order, of a sort, and acted like a proper officer, of a sort. *It must be some kind of God,* he told himself. *I would never do all this of my own choosing.*

Then came the celebrated Dark Day of May 19, 1780.

Seamus and his troops were quartered in Elizabethtown in the colony of New Jersey and did not personally see the "signs and wonders" reported in New England—the green and orange "saucers" or discs flying through the sky and the downpours of fish and frogs and eels that allegedly fell in many parts of Massachusetts and Connecticut.

In Elizabethtown, all that happened was the "supernatural" darkness that came in the middle of the day and then raised and disappeared as mysteriously as it had come. It had been an ordinary day until one in the afternoon, and then the dark started to fall. Seamus personally saw the chickens go to their roosts and heard the whippoorwills sing their sunset songs. At the darkest time, the troops had to light candles to see ahead of them, and so did the people in the houses of Elizabethtown. It was as black as midnight in a coal mine, although there had been no clouds gathering and no rain fell.

Day had simply turned into night at the wrong time and then corrected itself, as if it had discovered its error.

During the pitch-black hour, Seamus heard a dozen theological theories discussed among the troops—some on the verge of hysterical joy claimed God was warning the British of His wrath and others in hysterical terror weepingly proclaimed that God was actually in a fury against the Rebels. Seamus finally had to muster the troops, as the darkness slowly lifted, and give them a talk on eclipses and other natural phenomena and said even if he couldn't explain this particular phenomenon there was undoubtedly some scientific explanation that would be published shortly.

He didn't tell them about the time he saw a rock fall out of the sky and the scientists, instead of explaining it, simply said it had never happened. He was concerned with ending the hysteria, not with sharing his own private thoughts.

Later—months later—he heard about the religious zealots in New England who had gathered disciples and marched up into the hills to await the Second Coming of Christ. They must have had silly expressions when the darkness passed and Christ was nowhere to be seen, he thought. But evidently eels and frogs had fallen out of the sky: There were thousands and thousands who had collected bushels of the creatures, all over New England.

Personally, Seamus took the Dark Day, like the falling rock from nowhere, as evidence that science could not explain all of the world any more than religion could. We know very little really, he thought, but we are all enormously conceited.

He often wondered what Washington thought of the Dark Day. The man who had seen a star land on Earth, and a man get out of the star and talk to him, was probably less startled by darkness at noon than anyone else in the colonies. General Washington lived in a world where anything was possible.

And that, Seamus thought, *is probably why he believes he can win this war, and why he somehow keeps convincing the rest of us that, by Christ, maybe he can.*

But then came the mutiny of May twenty-fifth.

Seamus and his Fighting Irish were summoned urgently to a place called Basking Ridge. Naturally, they all thought they were going into battle again and they started out with the usual show of high spirits that soldiers use to keep up morale and hide their anxieties. At Basking Ridge, they found they were part of a large assembly brought together to overcome a Connecticut regiment that was in open mutiny.

When Seamus and his troops arrived, the Connecticut men—who looked, and claimed they were, even more famished by hunger than the rest of the Army— were already surrounded, front and rear, by two other regiments that had been called out to bring them back to order. Officers of the mutinous regiment were addressing the rebellious troops, some trying to subdue them with threats and curses, others arguing reasonably and offering promises that food was on its way.

One officer even claimed a herd of cattle had just arrived and that all would feast as never before.

"Go butcher them yourself," cried a skeptical Connecticut voice.

Seamus conferred with the other officers. Nobody wanted to shoot the mutineers—the army was dwindling fast enough from illness and desertions—but nobody could find the words to bring the starving men to accept military orders again. A Colonel Sumner said he thought the Yankees were half-crazy with chronic malnutrition.

Various of the mutineers were shouting to the regiments surrounding them, "Join us, lads, and we can all go home."

Another officer went forward and made a speech to the Yankees. He told them they would all be hanged tomorrow if they did not lay down their guns upon the instant.

"Bugger yourself," a voice shouted in reply. Otherwise there was sullen silence.

"Sir," Seamus said to Colonel Stewart of the Pennsylvania Line, "I cannot perceive a leader among these men, at all, at all. Is that not interesting?"

"What do you mean, sir?"

"They are remembering the rule that only the leader gets hanged. So there is no leader. Do you get my drift, sir?"

"They are cunning rascals, but what of it?"

"Colonel," Seamus said simply. "They are starved and driven past all endurance, but they have not taken leave of their senses. They know their situation is hopeless here. They know enough of battle by now to know what it means to be surrounded. They probably even know that more regiments are coming to make their situation more hopeless. We do not have to persuade them and we do not have to threaten them further. We only have to wait them out.''

Other officers had been listening. They exchanged glances with one another and with Colonel Stewart.

"The Irishman is your lad for crafty dealing," Stewart said finally. "What they really need, I suppose, is an excuse to surrender.''

"Wait them out," Seamus repeated. "Give them a few hours to mull over their predicament. Then promise amnesty to all. They'll march back to their quarters.''

And so it came to pass, and General Washington wrote an account of the incident for Congress, renewing his pleas for more food, and more food finally came—for a while.

Seamus always believed the mysterious Dark Day had been part of the reason for the mutiny: It is bad enough to be starved and exhausted and shot at and frozen, but when Nature itself seems to go mad, the spirits of men are truly broken and they are ready to join a stampede like frightened cattle. Seamus himself had considered the hypothesis that the Dark Day was just Nature's God's own cute way of announcing again that He did not give a fig for Mr. Jefferson's notion that He had endowed men with inalienable rights.

Then came the news of the treason of General Arnold and his conspiracy with the English Major Andre. As the news spread through the troops, gloom spread with it. Seamus knew that to most of the men the actions of Arnold meant that one of those who was closest to Washington and knew most about the overall situation now believed the British were sure to win.

Seamus was in Tappan when Andre was hanged. The man certainly was fearless as he climbed the gallows, Seamus had to admit, and, sure, from his point of view, he had only been doing his duty—like Captain Hale, the American spy the British had hanged earlier in the war.

"He made a brave end to it," Seamus said to Lieutenant O'Mara.

"That he did," said the Lieutenant. "But it's God's pity he didn't die peacefully in his bed two weeks before he ever sat down to plot with General Arnold."

"Aye," Seamus said sadly, "When a man of Arnold's rank turns the colors of his coat, it makes a man wonder if we still have any chance of winning at all, at all."

And then there were more forced marches and more battles, but the tide was turning. The French king had finally committed himself. The troops of his country, after landing in Rhode Island, moved rapidly south and suddenly the Americans found themselves actually winning battles instead of just winning in surprise hit-them-and-leave-them skirmishes and losing all the battles.

By 1781 it was obvious that the major struggles ahead were all going to be in the southern colonies, and with their French allies and better weather the Continentals began to experience hope again. Seamus became very aware that General Washington was not only a superb master of not losing when the odds were against him, but actually was now showing the additional talent of winning decisively when the odds shifted in his favor. *Faith*, he thought, *the man doesn't lose when he loses but he bloody well wins it all when he wins*.

In August, when the troops were conveyed by ship across Chesapeake Bay to Annapolis, Seamus and his troops all dined well and all had a few healthy jugs of rum to warm their spirits. The Dark Day was the bottom, the last pit of Hell, Seamus thought as the rum heated his brain, and from now on it is all uphill again.

After a few days, while Washington smoked herbs and listened to the opinions of all his officers and of the French officers as well, the troop ships were sent down the James River into Virginia.

The James River, Seamus thought: It might be an omen. "James River" would be *Anna Seamus* in Gaelic, as if it were named after himself. That either means good luck, or bad luck—or it doesn't mean a bloody thing. He was not sure he believed in omens, but he was not totally sure he didn't.

The land around the James River seemed the most beautiful Seamus has ever seen, outside Ireland. And we are here, he thought, to fill it with shot and shell and bloodshed.

At Williamsburg, Seamus met an old acquaintance—General Lafayette, looking fit and enthusiastic and no longer an outlaw since France officially entered the war.

"And have you been disturbed by any more Quakers and their strange speechifying?" Seamus asked the General after they had exchanged courtesies.

"Not a whit," said the Frenchman. "But I realize that my English teacher taught me the wrong brand of English for this continent. Have you tried to converse with any of the Vermonters? I hardly credit my ears."

Seamus grinned. "I have grown accustomed to all the New England accents," he said, "but I remain baffled by the speech of some of the Southern troops."

On the twenty-eighth of September General Washington ordered the troops to march on Yorktown to pay a visit to Lord Cornwallis, who was encamped there with—for once in the war—fewer troops than Washington and the French planned to send against him. Washington expected to drive the British back to their ships and put the southern colonies firmly under the control of the rebel Army. It might mark a significant turning point in the war—and those Whigs in the English Parliament who were demanding negotiations to end the prolonged hostilities might make good use of such an American victory as a debating point, the Whig position being that it would prove impossible to govern the colonies against their will.

Seamus did not expect at all what was to happen. There was no rational reason under heaven to expect it.

The troops marched toward Yorktown, and Seamus thought again and again that these were the most beautiful woodlands in all America. It was warm, but not hot, and everybody had received good rations since their arrival in Virginia. Seamus thought his troops would perform even better than was their habit. It was encouraging to be free of hunger and cold and to be adequately dressed for the climate.

Halfway to Yorktown, Washington even allowed the troops to stop and rest. Food and drink were provided. *For once,* Seamus thought, *we are not going into battle half-starved and half-dead from fatigue.*

The word came down when all were refreshed: The march would resume. Washington's order was that, if a British unit came out of Yorktown to meet them, his troops would exchange only one round and then charge rapidly, using their bayonettes to decide the issue.

Oh, he is a lovely man, Seamus thought, and cute as the devil's grandmother. The English Army had never really learned to use bayonettes, which their officers tended to regard as barbarous. Seamus wasn't sure about the French, but he knew full well that the Yankees and South-

erners and his own Irish troops were not squeamish about
bayonette usage and were all well practiced in the art.

Lord Cornwallis turned out to be a cute man, too. The
British did not march out to meet the overwhelming mass
of Continental and French troops moving in on Yorktown.
Cornwallis was going to stage a classical defense from
within the town itself, since it is harder to defeat an army
encamped in a town than one out in the open in a field.

Seamus knew that Washington would take Yorktown,
and Lord Cornwallis would eventually flee. In reason, that
had to happen. In reason, it would be an important moral
victory for the Rebels, but nothing beyond that—nothing
truly momentous—could be expected.

Washington began the seige in classical fashion. The
engineers were instructed to dig parallel trenches at fixed
distances from the fortress fronting Yorktown. This work
was to go forth under cover of night, while various small
deployments of troops pretended to be attacking the city
from the opposite side, across the marshlands. The ruse
worked: The British spent the first night firing toward the
handful of guerrillas in the marshes and woke in the morning to discover that a series of trenches and "saps"—
smaller trenches, connecting the major trenches—formed
a zigzag pattern leading to a major trench six hundred
yards from the fort and well supplied with cannon.

Seamus and his troops had assisted the engineers and
witnessed a very queer event indeed. It happened while
they were laying out their maps and planning the order of
the digging. An officer, unusually tall, suddenly appeared
among them, asked questions about the work, made suggestions, and seemed in a state of intense but well-
controlled excitement. The engineers, who had never seen
the commander-in-chief, did not know who this hulking
giant was, but Seamus recognized George Washington at
once, and softly, when out of earshot of the others, re-

monstrated with him for placing himself in such close proximity to the British guns.

"You are an Irishman and you saw a rock fall out of the sky," Washington said flatly and tonelessly. "You will understand this later."

Then, when the final decisions were made about the zigzag of the trenches, General Washington stepped forward—he had a lurching gait again, Seamus noted—and seized a pick-axe, struck exactly three blows to begin the first trench, and then said, "You may proceed, gentlemen."

He then walked back toward camp, stonefaced and inscrutible.

Knock. Knock. Knock.
—Who comes here?
—The son of a poor widow lady, seeking Light.

Bejesus, Seamus thought, *I will never understand that man fully, but I know this much: This is not just another battle.* General Washington was symbolically digging a grave for an enemy, or a pit for foes to fall into, or something like that. It was Sorcery, and it was bloody spooky business indeed. Seamus, who knew the General had once talked to an alien who flew about in a star like the fairies of Connemara, felt chills on his spine and thought his hairs must be literally bristling.

Cornwallis, once he perceived the zigzag trenches leading insidiously in the direction of his fort, increased the men in his own forward trenches and ordered heavy fire in the direction of the Rebel trenches. The Americans, moving about invisibly in their zigzags, did not even bother returning the compliment, since Washington wished to conserve munitions as long as possible. The work went on, and in three days the trench system for the seige of Yorktown was one of the classic seige trench designs of military history—the last classic of its kind, because soon new weapons would redefine the whole art of beseiging a fortified city.

When Washington had the trenches he wanted, where he wanted them, word came down to the troops that the first assault would soon be ordered and they should be in readiness. Washington chose as his signal for the attack the hoisting of the American flag at the forward battery.

When the flag went up, the Southerners unleashed barbaric yelps like demons from hell, the French shouted in English "Huzzah for the Americans," the Yankees shouted "Liberty or death," and Seamus's troops cried *"Sasanach ithean cac."* Then they all charged the first British redoubt, while their cannons opened fire on the city. General Washington in his commander's tent—with the famous four-poster bed that folded up for easy mobility during marches—knocked three times on his table, solemnly.

It was the only time in the war that Seamus literally felt a ball come so close to his head that he could hear it break the air as it passed. He had always thought stories of such "hairsbreadth" shots were myths. As usual with battle, he remembered little else, except howls and screams and smoke and then the wonderful joy when the British began to retreat and he realized he had gotten through another charge without being killed or wounded. Then, as usual, there was the tedious business of collecting corpses and arranging burials.

But the Brits were moving back, and the Americans were moving forward.

The seige continued remorselessly for several days. Yorktown was now surrounded on all sides—except at the rear, where Cornwallis could still retreat by crossing the York River. The pincers slowly closed on the town, and the trench system was working as it should: There were relatively few American or French casualties. The new forward trenches were now three hundred yards closer to the fort and the city. The only question was when Cornwallis would give up Yorktown and retreat.

On October fourteenth, Lieutenant O'Mara took a shot full in the face during a charge on the fort. Seamus leaped from his horse and rushed to the fallen man, but it was too late to even say a kind word to a departing spirit. O'Mara was faceless and brainless, having only some hair and a chin above the neck.

"Good-bye, Brian," Seamus said quietly. "I hope there's lots of whiskey and pretty colleens wherever you've gone."

Seamus returned to his horse, dry-eyed and not thinking at all, at all. He had seen too many of his men die to feel anything anymore when it happened again, except for a terrible emptiness where his emotions used to be.

"*Sasanach ithean cac,*" he screamed, and the charge continued.

The battle pressed forward each day and the Rebels soon owned all the land fronting on Yorktown. Cornwallis made his attempt to retreat two days later, on October sixteenth. Seamus and all the American troops knew about it, because their forward redoubts could now see what was going on in the town, and reported that the British troops were being marched to the ships to cross the York River and begin a retreat.

Well, Seamus thought, *we've won that town—but how many more battles still wait ahead before this bloody business is over?*

As night fell, the forward redoubts reported that the British were ready to set sail. The Americans could enter Yorktown in the morning, unopposed, and would hold strategic command of the southern colonies.

It was a turning point, but nobody thought it was the end.

And then the rains came. Out of a clear sky, clouds as black as the slaves and as sudden as the knife throwing of the southern troops. A deluge such as Seamus had never seen before, even in the worst of Ireland's rainy season. And winds like the wrath of God.

Some of the men insisted it was the "hurrikan," that Caribbean terror that sometimes afflicted the colonies. Others denied that it was a true "hurrikan" and claimed it was only the most terrific rainstorm of the century.

Oh, bejesus, Seamus thought, *General Washington has been knock-knock-knocking again.*

Whatever it was, the British retreat was impossible. The ship's captains all agreed that sailing in that wind was certain suicide. The Americans and French quickly moved in to surround Yorktown while the British troops were on the ships or waiting orders on the docks. The pincers had closed as rain had joined the French and American pressure on the tactical ingenuity of Lord Cornwallis.

The rain continued all night, and the British were trapped between the enemy armies and an escape route that was now closed by what appeared an act of God to the pious. The following morning, the seventeenth, Cornwallis sent a negotiating party to Washington to confer on the terms of surrender.

And all Seamus could think, as the negotiations dragged on, was that maybe he had seen an act of God after all. Maybe Nature's God moved more subtly and slowly than he had realized earlier. Maybe, by Christ, Nature's God really did intend the world to recognize that all men were created equal and all were entitled to life, liberty, and the pursuit of happiness. Maybe, by Christ, Mr. Jefferson was not just a great poet or a sorcerer but a true prophet. And maybe, if it could happen here, it could happen in Ireland, too . . .

Of course, one part of his mind—the alien he called "James Moon," the one who had read too many books—did not believe such extravagant metaphysical theories could be deduced from one lucky rainstorm. But James Moon was a fading voice now; Colonel Seamus Muadhen was the dominant half of that partnership—and what is an Irish soldier without a superstition and a myth to guide him?

On October nineteenth, Lord Cornwallis formally surrendered to General Washington. Moved by some whimsey that has puzzled historians since, Cornwallis ordered his military band to play *The World Turned Upside Down* as he handed over his sword.

Colonel Muadhen was impatient to receive his final pay. He now, finally, had a reason to return to Ireland: George III had more lessons to learn about what men will endure for life, liberty, and the pursuit of happiness, and the place to teach him was Ireland, the misfortunate land that had been colonized centuries before any part of America or Asia or Africa, the first of England's raped and mutilated victims.

Seamus set sail on November twenty-fifth and arrived in Dingle Bay a few days before Christmas. One of the first things he saw was a newspaper headline:

TRAGEDY STRIKES MEMBER OF PARLIAMENT
BABCOCK FAMILY BEREAVED

Oh, Jesus, Seamus thought, this is the worst possible time for me to be reminded that the English are human beings, too, and suffer as all of us suffer. He threw the paper down. He did not want to know what had happened to his former employers.

11. The Grand Orient and Other Treacheries

Paris—Strasbourg 1781

A dagger with a handle like flame
and on it the initials, S.B.

By the time the news arrived in Paris that Lord Cornwallis had actually surrendered to the ragged rabble of American rebels at Yorktown on October nineteenth, it was already December sixth. The Duke of Orleans nonetheless announced a ball at his Paris mansion that evening and, of course, all of his hundred most intimate enemies were there, including the odious M. Gabriel Sartines, the cunning little spymaster whose role in the government was increasingly undefined but distinctly growing in power every time the moon changed.

There was no way Orleans could have a party without Sartines planting a few agents among the guests. Orleans thought it would be amusing to have the damned fishmonger's son there in person, so he sent him an engraved invitation. "While he watches me," Orleans thought craftily, "I will also be watching him." It did not occur to him that the rooster might have had similarly Machiavellian delusions when he invited the fox into the chicken coop.

Although Orleans, as host, circulated politely and greeted everybody warmly, he did manage to spend much of his time within earshot of the crafty and cunning little man the underworld called Sardines, and who was wearing, as usual, the most expensive wig in the room. Birth shows, Orleans thought, the damned little upstart must flaunt the most costly of everything, to remind himself that he can almost pass as a gentleman.

Naturally, the defeat of the British Empire by the barbaric Americans was the main topic of conversation, as Orleans had expected. The duke had instructed his musicians to begin the evening's entertainment with *The World Turned Upside Down*, the song Cornwallis had had his army band play as he surrendered his sword to Washington. Orleans also used every opportunity to philosophize about the decline of the Roman Empire and ask if the American victory were the first sign of a similar decline of the British Empire; that line of thought led easily into contemplation of the impermanence of all political institutions and the Law of Change that destroys all who are not shrewd enough to move with the times and adapt to new circumstances. An Enlightened Monarch like the Emperor Joseph of Austria understood that, Orleans hinted gently, but England's George III had suffered the delusion that Absolute Monarchy was still possible. He never explicitly drew the parallel with the stout young man in Versailles, of course. His listeners were left to think of that obvious lesson for themselves.

The seed was planted, and the inevitable sprouts appeared in conversations throughout the ballroom. On one of his returns to the vicinity of Minister Sartines, Orleans heard Madame de Monnier asking, ''Do you think we will ever have democracy in France, Gabriel?''

Sartines extended a quick little claw to snatch a canapé from a passing tray before he answered. "We have had every other mania," he said drily. "I dare not hope we will escape the latest. If we can swallow Theology, which asks us to believe three equals one, we can make one more leap of mathematical imagination and accept the Democratic dogma that asks us to believe any digit equals any other digit."

"You shock me," Madame said. "I thought you were a liberal by conviction."

"I am unconvinced by conviction," said Sartines. "The totally convinced and the totally stupid have too much in common for the resemblence to be accidental. And, besides, convictions grow more expensive lately. I fear they are luxuries few of us can afford these days. You must remember I am a monarchist by profession."

"You flaunt your cynicism?" Madame exclaimed.

Sartines snatched another canapé quickly. "Cynicism and idealism are both boyish illusions," he said carefully. "To maintain either of those attitudes, you must ignore half of what you see and almost all of what you hear. In my profession I cannot afford to ignore anything. I dare not have philosophical attitudes, political convictions, or other illusions. I am cursed with realism."

"Is it a curse?" Madame asked archly.

"Worse than death. Ask any artist about that."

Orleans drawled carelessly, "But might it not prove to be realistic to assume democracy is inevitable?"

"I am sure of it," Sartines pronounced. "Paris can resist everything but fashions, and democracy is the fashion now."

"You are jaded," Madame declared. "I adore fashion. After all, it is all that saves us from the tedium of good taste and the monotony of common sense. The more outrageous a new fashion is, the more exciting I find it. I believe quite firmly in being a slave of fashion. What are offered as eternal truths or universal laws usually turn out to be local or temporal prejudices, or fashions, anyway, so why not have the latest style in everything? Besides, without fashion we might all become as dull as the British."

"I am not perfectly convinced of the dullness of the British," Sartines said. "Negotiating with them on government affairs sometimes gives me the distinct impression that their Foreign Office, at least, is approximately as dull as the great white shark or the barracuda."

"Oh, don't quarrel with my metaphors, Gabriel," Madame exclaimed. "Or my similes, I mean. The British are dull about all the important matters. Except for going mad once or twice a year, their king is a total bore, their food is dreadful, and they have to import composers from the Continent to have any music at all. I believe they even found their Mr. Handel somewhere in Germany."

"Oh, I quite share your preferences," Sartines said warmly. "Speaking personally, I much prefer gaudy Parisian fashions to neat British bank ledgers. I also prefer thrilling new fads to irremediable old facts and a seat at the theatre to my grubby bureaucratic desk. All amusing and fantastic things have glamour, just like the new styles in gowns and furs you adore, which I also enjoy artistically, since they make even beautiful women as bizarre and sinister as the ugly ones, and I enjoy Gothic ruins. The greatest operas I have ever seen were as splendid as the most outrageous lies

I have been told by ambassadors. Exquisitely contrived fantasies of all sorts have a transcendental radiance about them. It is my misfortune to have the task of looking behind every masque to see what the actors are really hatching. I repeat that I am cursed with the necessity of realism. And what is worse, none pity me. Will you at least pity me, Madame?''

While Madame decided whether to encourage that left-handed flirtation, Orleans interposed smoothly, ''I have often suspected that realism was the last thing to concern government officials.''

''Not at all, *mon duc,*'' Sartines replied quickly. ''It is merely the last thing we ever talk about.''

''Yes,'' said Orleans. ''I quite enjoyed the skill with which you deflected the conversation from the threat of democracy.''

''It is no threat to me, I assure you,'' said Sartines. ''Every government eventually finds it needs me, or men like me. My profession may only be the second oldest in time but it is the first in tenacity.''

But Madame decided to return the conversation to its first declivity. ''You still have not declared your private opinion, Gabriel. What do think after working hours, when you are not a monarchist by profession?''

Sartines seemed to reflect a moment. A servant quickly approached with the wine tray and he took a glass. ''The worst that can happen under monarchy is rule by a single imbecile,'' he said finally, ''but democracy often means the rule by an assembly of three or four hundred imbeciles.''

''Oh, come now—is one imbecile really much better than a houseful of them?'' Madame demanded.

''A single imbecile is merely an annoyance,'' Sartines said. ''One learns to maneuver around him. Four hundred imbeciles in solemn session together can be as inexorable as a river in flood. One cannot maneuver, one is carried by the momentum.''

Orleans thought it might be amusing to hear the loathesome Sartines defend that paradox, but it was his duty to circulate once again. He spoke to a dozen important men and their wives. All of the men did a marvelous job of hiding their contempt for him; he sincerely admired their performances. They were men who had (they thought) taken advantage of his wealth, his generosity, and his famous gullibility. They were all on his List. They would be too compromised by debt and other entanglements to resist him when the day came to remind them of their obligations. Meanwhile, it was amusing that the fools thought they had played him for a fool.

When the good *duc* returned to the vicinity of Sartines and Madame de Monnier, they had been joined by M. de Beaumarchais, who had the inevitable pretty little *demi-vierge* on his arm. In two or three minutes, Orleans reflected, we will be joined by her father, who knows (as all Paris knows) the nets Beaumarchais weaves around young girls. He will be wearing a suspicious frown, the father will, and that is how I will recognize him.

"Nobody can understand Dr. Cyprus," Beaumarchais was saying, "so everybody assumes he is profound. That is a favorite device with German philosophers, and it always seems to work."

"Cyprus gives me great pleasure," Sartines said. "The less I understand of a page of his, the more I enjoy it, because it is clear at least that he represents the kind of enemy of our existing social order that I, as a government official, need never fear. He is a sheep in wolves' clothing.

"Of course," Beaumarchais said. "You mean that

his ideas, if accepted, would persuade people to become reactionaries while thinking they are radicals.''

"He persuades his readers that the age of bubonic plague and witch burning was wonderful," Sartines said. "As long as people think that way, the present order will not be threatened radically, but only considered a little less wonderful than the Thirteenth Century."

"I suspect that some of your liberal convictions are still with you, Gabriel, even if you try to hide them," Madame remarked.

"I am merely being practical," Sartines said. "The Age of Faith was splendid for men of my calibre. Whenever a philosopher arises to denounce Reason as a whore, I know my profession remains secure."

"My suspicions increase," Madame said. "Your irony grows untypically obvious."

"To persons such as you, dear lady. I am only alarmed when the majority in any room does not cheerfully misunderstand my jokes," Sartines smiled pleasantly, and sipped some more wine.

"You prefer to be an enigma?" Orleans drawled. "I thought that was becoming passé."

Madame said, "Gabriel probably shares the male delusion that we women are attracted to enigmatic men. Not at all, we are attracted to men who think *we* are engimatic. That makes all the difference in the world."

"I defend my position," Sartines declared promptly. "An accepted definition is every bit as serious as a legal sentence. Worse: it can be as fatal as medical diagnosis, which, as you know, often kills the patient. The greatest art is cryptic. The best music is totally ineffable. A predictible joke is not funny. The most wonderful affaires are those in which both parties suspect the other of deception but can never prove it. It is doubt, not faith, that makes life worth living. Paradox is all.''

Beaumarchais shook his head dubiously, and said, ''You are shrewd about most things, Gabriel, but not about love. In my experience, the most delicious affaires have been not those with the greatest amount of deception—women do that just for deviltry, bless them—but those affaires in which the deception is urgently necessary. This provides that extra thrill that prevents conquest from degenerating to boredom. It is even more exciting when there is a jealous husband to provide the real chance that one might be stabbed climbing out the window at dawn.''

An elderly marquis from the south appeared with a suspicious frown. He hovered behind Beaumarchais's little girl-woman. *I was right,* Orleans thought. *That is the protective father I expected.*

Sartines meanwhile was disagreeing with M. Beaumarchais. ''For me, the greatest pleasures are those that leave one mildly dissatisfied and always longing for just a little bit more. Like caviar, for instance, or the music of Mozart—or political power, to take the extreme example. Or that marvelous new snuff with crushed coca leaves in it. Have you sampled it? A taste of paradise on earth, I assure you. We are destroyed when we become satisfied; it is the Bog of Apathy, which leads downward to the abyss of senility and death. When a man becomes satisfied, it is because he thinks only of the safe and useful. He should be deported to England to open a grocery shop.''

''You express it so well,'' Madame said. ''I think it is my vices and follies that keep me young, and prudence that makes most shallow women grow old. I find it dreadful that some persons nowadays expect even the king himself to serve some useful function. In my day it was enough that he provided an amusing subject of scandal.''

The elderly marquis frowned more balefully but said nothing.

Beaumarchais sighed lugubriously. ''Utility is the tyrant of our time,'' he said to Sartines. ''Nowadays even we playwrights are expected to be significant, which is almost as tedious as being useful. The next thing you know, we will even be expected to be political.''

''Some have found significance in your comedies,'' Madame said drily. ''A few have even suspected the presence of politics.''

''I deny it vehemently,'' Beaumarchais declared. ''Any fool can be indignant about politics. My talent is to be sardonic. An obtuse age like this does not appreciate the difference. If I had foreseen Parisian audiences of today, I would have become a musician or a chef. Musicians are only expected to heat the blood, like a good cognac, and chefs merely have to be insolent.''

''It is worse than that,'' Sartines commented. ''My wife says that she is sincerely grateful, these days, if the chef refrains from poisoning us outright. The sauces one encounters at some salons make me think we might as well be living in Belgium.''

''Oh?'' Beaumarchais cocked an eyebrow. ''You still see your wife occasionally?''

''Not as often as you do,'' Sartines said. ''But, unlike most Parisian couples, we are still on speaking terms. She finds my government position useful in her quest for amusing new lovers and I am still as enthralled as ever by her truly astounding ability to lie with a straight face.''

"I was correct earlier," Madame said. "You *are* a cynic."

Sartines made a gesture of despair. "I will fight to the death against being defined or labeled. The unexamined life may not be worth living, but the defined and explicated life is not even worth talking about. I once knew a wild Neapolitan who escaped from the Bastille, but no man in history has ever escaped from a definition. It is more fatal than a judicial verdict, as I said before. Without duplicity, one might as well be a specimen in a laboratory jar."

Orleans tried to keep an impassive face, but he involuntarily stared at Sartines, to see if the little trickster was covertly watching him to observe his reaction to the carefully oblique reference to Sigismundo Celine in the middle of that flight of irony. Sartines, however, was not looking in his direction at all. Orleans relaxed, and told himself not to become nervous and imaginative at this stage of the game. He was not aware that Beaumarchais, who worked for Sartines part time, had been instructed to watch his reaction to the story of the man who escaped the Bastille, and had carefully noted his reflex tension and relaxation.

"I can bear my wife's company occasionally," Orleans said, working hard at being bland. "That is because she has never deceived me."

Madame exclaimed, clapping her hands, "A Frenchman whose wife has never deceived him? Next we will hear of a pig with wings, or a religious Pope."

"She has never deceived me because I have never trusted her," Orleans said calmly. "The difference between a happy marriage and an affaire is that people in affaires get so carried away by passion that each believes the drivel the other utters."

But Madame was intrigued by the quickly elided

mystery, which fascinated her more than carefully cultivated witticisms. "There was a man who actually escaped the Bastille, Gabriel? That must be an extraordinary story."

"It is an annoying story, rather," Sartines said. "I never did get to the bottom of it, and nothing vexes me more than unsolved mysteries. Some nights I still lie awake and speculate about it." He turned to Orleans, as if seeking help. "Can you not introduce a new topic? No government official likes to talk about his failures."

"I do not believe you ever fail," Orleans said. "I would imagine you merely have to wait longer to spring your trap in some cases than in others. I do not underestimate you, monsieur."

"First I am called a cynic," Sartines said to the group. "Now I am accused of infallibility. What have I ever done to become such an object of dread?"

The little virgin princess spoke up suddenly. "People say you are the head of the spy bureau for the king," she said. "Is that true?"

"My dear young lady," Sartines said. "That is a shocking remark. Other countries may have spies, but France merely has good friends who keep their eyes and ears open."

"Precisely," Beaumarchais said. "Other nations have gross injustices, but we only have unresolved social problems."

"Some noble ladies are no better than whores," Madame said, "but I have merely retained my capacity for Romance."

"Some men are treacherous," Sartines added, "but I merely avoid being too obvious."

The young girl was frowning as much as her father

now. "You people are making an art of glamorizing evil things. That is not amusing. It is hypocrisy."

"And what, pray, is wrong with hypocrisy?" Madame asked. "A world without hypocrites, like a world without good manners, would be rude and crude and quite insufferable."

"Hypocrisy, not democracy, is the great equalizer," Beaumarchais added. "It is the only art most people can practice with any real skill. Expert hypocrites are more common than great musicians or tolerable painters. The art of hypocrisy, in fact, is essential to diplomacy or true courtesy. I am constantly amazed that even fools and scoundrels are accomplished at this one most democratic of all arts: sincere hypocrisy."

"It is so popular precisely because it is so easy, I think," the girl said angrily. "Morality is much more difficult, is it not?"

"It is not only difficult, but pointless," Madame pronounced. "What are the social consequences, if the world even suspects that you have become moral? Intelligent persons avoid you, and some insufferable parish priest comes around to warn you against the sin of pride."

"Do not be too quick to dismiss morality utterly, Madame," Sartines said. "Like hypocrisy, it has its purposes. It was invented, I have long believed, to stave off boredom. Without morality, many of our favorite vices would eventually become tedious. Morality prevents that by giving us the thrill of always feeling sinful."

"All the advantage still seems to be on the side of hypocrisy," Orleans commented.

"Not at all," Sartines said. "Hypocrisy is merely the lies we tell others, which is a social lubricant in high cultures like ours. Morality is the lies we tell ourselves, which can prove fatal eventually. That is why I warn young people to never let their conscience be their guide. It is a worse liar than vanity, to which it is probably related.''

"True morality," the young lady declared firmly, "is based entirely on the love of God. You people would not understand that."

"Indeed, I do not," Madame said. *"Fear* of God, yes; that is comprehensible. The Old Testament makes quite clear that He is a dirty old Jew. That contemptible impression is confirmed by the fact that He maliciously intermingled the organs of love with the urinary tract. And there is also the little joke He plays on us poor women once a month. Considering such vulgarities, I suspect that His absolute power has corrupted Him, as happened with the equally gross Caligula.''

"I will not listen to such blasphemy and cynicism a moment longer," the young lady said, flouncing off. The father glared at everybody and followed her.

"You have lost a conquest," Sartines said to Beaumarchais.

"Not at all. She will be back, eventually, to try to reform me. Girls of that type believe all men can be reformed."

"And men of your type," Orleans said, "believe that all girls like her can be corrupted."

"In this world," Madame de Monnier said calmly, "the contest is unequal and the outcome predictible."

The party ended at midnight; Sartines and Beaumarchais left separately, Sartines taking his coach and Beaumarchais strolling off in the opposite direction. Beaumarchais walked toward a new faubourg that

was still largely unsettled. He came to a large empty
lot and walked to the far side, stopping suddenly to
urinate against a tree. At the same time, he studied
the lot and the street he had just departed. Finished,
he darted quickly into an alley and walked much more
rapidly. Anybody who had been following him had
prudently stayed far back when he entered the lot, and
was now too far behind to catch up.

That empty lot game was standard procedure for
anybody meeting Minister Sartines on confidential
business at midnight. "I only run the official spy network in this country," Sartines told his men. "Do not
ever imagine I run the *only* spy network."

Beaumarchais arrived at Sartines's house at the time
they had arranged beforehand. Over their cognac, they
compared notes and agreed that only one thing was sure:
The Duke of Orleans was still frightened of the elusive
and mysterious Neopolitan, Sigismundo Celine, who appeared to have vanished off the face of the earth in 1772.

"Whatever has happened to Signor Celine," Sartines said, "we can be sure Orleans did not have him
murdered. Louis Phillipe d'Orleans is many things,
but he is not a man to be frightened of ghosts."

Sartines and Beaumarchais were as oblivious as Orleans of the singular fact that Sigismundo Celine had
been at the party with them, nine years older than when
Sartines had last seen him and suitably disguised.

Orleans, however, was thinking of that strange and
melodramatic possibility, not without symptoms of
vertigo, while Sartines and Beaumarchais finished their
cognacs and bade each other a good night.

Louis Phillipe d'Orleans, "the friend of the people," the nation's most famous philanthropist and liberal, was, in fact, uneasily contemplating a dagger that
he had just found neatly stuck to the hilt in the center

of his pillow, as he retired for bed. It was expensive and had many jewels and was not the sort of toy a man would casually leave behind, a dagger with a handle like flame and on it the initials S.B.

Sigismundo Balsamo, Orleans thought. *He is deliberately reminding us of that, of his Sicilian bandit father. He wants us to think of the blood oaths and vendettas and the Mafia and Satanic covens and everything that makes the Kingdom of Naples and Sicily seem barbarous to us. And frightening to us.*

He has returned at last and he wants to seem like an avenging demon out of a nightmare.

Sigismundo's half-brother, Guiseppe Balsamo, known to most of Europe as "Count Cagliostro," was the subject of an extensive file in the locked cabinet of Gabriel de Sartines.

Sartines was well aware that, unknown to most people except its own members, the largest of all Freemasonic orders had been formed in France in the last decade—the Grand Orient Lodge of Egyptian Freemasonry. He knew that Cagliostro was the principal recruiter and figurehead for the Grand Orient. Sartines was also fairly sure that the actual financial backing for Cagliostro's "Egyptian" cult came from the Duke of Orleans. He was deeply suspicious that this whole contraption was part of a long-range plan to raise Orleans to the throne of France.

But Sartines was also strongly of the opinion that something else was involved in the Grand Orient— something that went beyond politics in the normal sense—and that the whole mystery somehow linked back to Naples, where both Cagliostro and the mysterious Sigismundo Celine had their origins. And it was linked to Poussin's painting, *The Shepherds of Ar-*

cadia, which King Louis XVI kept in a private suite separate from the rest of the royal art collection, and with the motto, *Et in Arcadia Ego,* which appeared in that painting and in the Grand Orient's "Egyptian" initiation rituals. Worse yet, it was also linked—Sartines was convinced—to the Jacobite wars in England and Ireland and to Charles Radclyffe, the illegitimate son of Charles II of England, who had founded the Strict Observance Rite of Freemasonry, out of which the Grand Orient had emerged.

Of all the paradoxes and jokes Sartines had uttered at Orleans's home that night, he had allowed himself one sentence of pure truth: Unsolved mysteries vexed him and he did lie awake at night puzzling over them. That night, as on many others, he stared at the ceiling, trying to get to sleep, and thought again about how Orleans's dynastic ambitions were linked to the wars between the Scotsman, James II, and the Dutchman, William of Orange, over which of them should be king of England, and how such a web could include, crucially, an obscure Neapolitan music student like Sigismundo Celine, who had been clapped in the Bastille for unknown reasons, escaped miraculously, was recaptured and then vanished as if he had gone to the moon.

Three shepherds looking at a grave: That was the subject of the mysterious painting the king kept hidden. Three shepherds and a tombstone marked *Et in Arcadia Ego.* Three shepherds, Sartines thought again; and some link with the three ruffians who killed the Widow's Son in the Freemasonic legend: Jubela, Jubelo, Jubelum. Why three? Why do Freemasons say, "Greetings on all three sides of the triangle"? So many things come in threes, he thought perplexedly. Yesterday, today, and tomorrow; past, present, and future;

height, width, and depth. The Three Wise Men at the stable in Bethelehem. The three sons of Noah—Ham, Shem, and Japhet. Three meals a day. Damnation, I am going in circles. Three shepherds and a grave make four. Three times four is twelve. The twelve signs of the Zodiac. The twelve labors of Hercules. The twelve apostles of Jesus.

At six in the morning, Sartines was still awake, wondering why juries have twelve members and eggs are sold by the dozen and why all coinages from Babylon to the present were based on a duodecimal system and why the zodiac and the profane calendar do not correspond but each is yet divided into twelve parts.

He dozed off dreaming of the ramifications of the consternation of the fornification of the population in the cooperation of the procrastination of the monsturbation of the castroidclownation of the incamination for the phartification on the pantification with the hulahulalation of a warp in process.

In Strasbourg, the whole town was talking about the latest miracles of the legendary Count Cagliostro. Twice a week, in the town square, the two thousand-year-old wizard healed the ill, curing dozens and scores at a time. And the marvelous count did this while using no drugs or medicines, but merely by walking among the sick, talking softly and touching them, transferring his "spiritual magnetism," as he called it, into their bodies.

Of course, a few of the local physicians fumed and spoke heatedly of "charlatanry" and "fraud," but nobody took them very seriously. Almost everyone seemed to know somebody who had been healed, and the doctors certainly could not explain that. In fact, when the skeptics did try to explain, it was obvious to every Jacques and his brother that they were talking in empty phrases to conceal their own ignorance. The "spiritual magnetism" was real—many who did not need healing had nonetheless *felt* the energy merely by being among the curious onlookers.

One lone Dominican fanatic offered an explanation that people might have believed and understood—Black Magic. But that monk had been silenced by Cardinal de Rohan, who soon became known as one of the most fervent admirers and protectors of the wonder-worker who looked like a thirty-year-old Italian but claimed to be a two thousand-year-old Arab who had known Jesus personally in Galilee and learned his arts from that Divine Source. While Cardinal de Rohan never spoke about that somewhat touchy issue, he had let it be known that there was no Heresy or Witchcraft in the Count, who was a man of pious motives, working only to heal the sick for the greater glory of God.

In fact, although he did not talk about it in public, Prince Louis René Edouard Guemenée, Cardinal de Rohan, was more concerned with Count Cagliostro's other talents than with all those gaudy public healings of riffraff and common scum. The cardinal had actually seen the Great Work—the Magnum Opus—with his own eyes, a year ago in 1780. It was obvious to a man of the world, such as the cardinal, that the count was so unworldly and devout that he himself never realized the enormous profits to be made on that line of work, but de Rohan was convinced that, with time and patience, even the saintly Cagliostro could be made to see the more practical side of such matters.

The Great Work had hardly interested Count Cagliostro at all: When he had first mentioned that it was among the arts he knew, the remark had been casual and he had seemed puzzled when the cardinal, a man of God, had insisted on asking for details. The Transformation was part of the training for more spiritual work, Cagliostro had explained, and it did not have nearly the importance that greedy materialists placed upon it. Just when the cardinal was beginning to suspect that all this had some of the earmarks of a mountebank's tales, Cagliostro said he would be glad to demonstrate the trivial matter if the cardinal's curiosity were scientific only and not mercenary. He said it with such childish innocence that the prince cardinal de Rohan almost thought the man must be an imbecile.

Nonetheless, the Count had demonstrated the Great Work, and he had done it in the cardinal's own study, without any modern devices, using only the primitive smithy's furnace that the medieval alchemists employed.

The cardinal had provided the lead himself, and always remembered that he had watched the whole Transformation most carefully and skeptically. Actually, the operation took nearly a whole day, but the cardinal never left the room, since he was not without awareness that some who act saintly are capable of being scoundrels when your back is turned. There was a slow fire of low temperature—"The Work must never be violent," Cagliostro said—and the smoke in the room was intense at times. Indeed, sitting there in the smoke, listening to the naive holy man ramble on about Judea two thousand years ago, and his friends on the planet Mars, and his oath of celibacy (taken in A.D. 33 at the express command of Our Saviour), and his visit to the New World with Saint Brendan, and the fact that anyone totally celibate for 333 years could perform the Transmutation, the cardinal found it hard not to doze at times, but he always forced himself to stay awake and alert, even when the count experimentally—to break the tedium—conveyed him on an astral journey to the planet Venus where the women were all green and walked about with no clothes, like Eve in Eden, because they had never known Sin or Shame.

The trip to Venus, in fact, was the most exciting part of the Great Work, because the count, although a holy man and a good storyteller, had a tendency to repeat himself a bit and even spoke in a lower and lower drone as the interminable Cosmic Furnace spewed out more and more strange vapors. The best thing about Venus was that those naked green women all had the gift of prophecy and one of them told the cardinal that his most secret desire would be granted if he told her what it was. And, because Venus was a place without sin or shame, he told her frankly of his great love for Marie Antoinette and his secret fantasy that some day, that love might be consummated.

And then Cagliostro guided him back to Earth and the Great Work was accomplished. Lead had indeed gone into the Cosmic Furnace, but gold came out. You can be sure the cardinal had experts examine the gold for purity the very next day, and it was of the highest quality.

Then the real power of alchemy began to manifest itself. The cardinal received a letter from the queen that was not only ardent but actually encouraging, and she wrote as if she had read his secret heart while he was unveiling it to the angel-women of Venus.

The cardinal was hooked, and Cagliostro slowly began reeling him in. After all, the letter had been the most dangerous part of the business; although a skillful forgery, it was still a forgery, and the Cardinal might have had further doubts at that point and instigated his own investigation into the matter. But the fool had gold, and expected more, and was now beyond reason. He was quite certain he was about to become the lover of the queen herself.

It is so easy to fleece them, Cagliostro thought, *that sometimes it almost bores me and I become impatient for the real work that lies ahead, when we are ready to teach Louis XVI what the Americans have just taught George III.*

Finding an actress who could pass as Marie Antoinette was soon accomplished. As long as the meeting was staged in a garden at night, a man as infatuated as the cardinal would easily be deceived.

All was running smoothly, as planned.

Then Cagliostro received two letters in the same post—from Ingolstadt and Paris. When he opened them, he found they were, as expected, from Weishaupt and Orleans. Both told of finding flame daggers—the ancient sign of the Order of Assassins—in their pillows. Both told him the initials on the daggers were S.B.

So, Cagliostro thought, *my dear brother, after long years of meditation, has decided to re-enter the game. I wonder when I will get my flame dagger.*

Then he started counting the years. Sigismundo would be thirty-one now: still young enough to be tough and sinewy if he had kept in shape (and he probably had), old enough and experienced enough in these games to be as tricky as a Chinese puzzle-box.

Nearly a month had to pass, and it was 1782, before Cagliostro decided that his own flame dagger of warning would not arrive for a long time—not until Sigismundo had kept him in suspense a sufficient time to be sure that the waiting was itself a form of torture.

Good, good, the count thought then with genuine

pleasure, he may be only a Neapolitan but he has
learned to play this game as well as we do it in Sicily.
The contest will be formidable.

Coming soon . . .
Volume 4 of the Historical Illuminati Chronicles,
THE WORLD TURNED UPSIDE DOWN